Matthew Jordan paused; Olivia waited impatiently

"And wives," he concluded.

"Wives—" she stared back in total incomprehension. "Wives," she repeated once again.

He continued to watch her over his glass, the expression in his eyes unreadable. "If you were my wife," he clarified, "you would qualify under the clause."

A mixture of horror and incredulity went through her at the very thought. "But I'm not," she said at last.

"You could be." She wondered if the wine had gone to her head or if he'd actually said what she'd thought. "What's that supposed to mean?" she asked.

He leaned toward her and elaborated slowly. "My dear Miss Garland, what it means is that I'm prepared to give you your company back. On one condition." He paused. "On condition that you agree to marry me."

STEPHANIE HOWARD is a British author whose two ambitions since childhood were to see the world and write. Her first venture into the world was a four-year stay in Italy, learning the language and supporting herself by writing short stories. Then her sensible side brought her back to London to read Social Administrations at the London School of Economics. She has held various editorial posts at magazines such as *Reader's Digest*, *Vanity Fair*, *Women's Own*, as well as writing free-lance for *Cosmopolitan*, *Good Housekeeping* and *The Observer*. However she has spent the past six years happily trotting around the globe. Last year she returned to the U.K. to write.

Books by Stephanie Howard

HARLEQUIN PRESENTS
1098—RELUCTANT PRISONER
1130—DARK LUCIFER
1168—HIGHLAND TURMOIL

Don't miss any of our special offers. Write to us at the following address for information on our newest releases.

Harlequin Reader Service
901 Fuhrmann Blvd., P.O. Box 1397, Buffalo, NY 14240
Canadian address: P.O. Box 603,
Fort Erie, Ont. L2A 5X3

STEPHANIE HOWARD

bride for a price

Harlequin Books

TORONTO • NEW YORK • LONDON
AMSTERDAM • PARIS • SYDNEY • HAMBURG
STOCKHOLM • ATHENS • TOKYO • MILAN

Harlequin Presents first edition June 1990
ISBN 0-373-11273-4

Original hardcover edition published in 1989
by Mills & Boon Limited

CHAPTER ONE

'THANK heavens for dear old dependable Lewis! How would I ever manage without him?'

Olivia frowned with concentration as she bent her shiny, neat dark head over the sheets of figures and statistics that the company's director-cum-accountant had thoughtfully prepared for her. Statistics and figures were not Olivia's strong point, as she was all too willing to concede, but right now she desperately needed to have these particular statistics at her fingertips. They were her armour and her strongest weapon in the battle that lay ahead.

As the office door opened, she glanced up, her blue eyes smiling at the tall, distinguished figure with the iron-grey hair who came into the room. 'Ready?' he asked her with a sympathetic nod. 'I think we ought to make a move.'

Olivia straightened. 'He hasn't arrived yet, has he?' In spite of herself, she felt a tremor of alarm.

But Lewis threw her a reassuring smile as he adjusted the cuffs of his immaculate dark suit and glanced at the slim gold watch at his wrist. 'Not yet, Miss Garland,' he confirmed. 'But the chauffeur radioed through just a couple of minutes ago. They should be here in less than a quarter of an hour.'

Olivia nodded. 'Good,' she said. And she

meant it, despite another slight flutter of nerves. She had been trying to arrange this meeting for more than two months, and she could even now scarcely believe that the accursed Matthew Jordan, the man who was currently blighting her life, had finally deigned to make the journey to Chester to meet her face to face.

She stood up, pushing aside the sheets of bewildering data that she had been poring over for the past couple of hours. If she didn't know it now, she never would.

She smoothed the slim skirt of the deep navy suit she wore and nervously touched the high-buttoned collar of the contrasting cream silk crêpe-de-Chine blouse. With her glossy dark hair, wide-set deep blue eyes and flawless ivory complexion, the colours were discreetly flattering—while the neat chignon and precise, tailored lines of her clothes helped to project a professional image. An image she was fervently hoping effectively masked her inner turmoil.

She glanced gratefully at Lewis. Thank heavens she had him on her side! 'Is everything ready?' she enquired.

'Just as we planned, Miss Garland. Come and have a look for yourself.'

Olivia followed him to the door, smiling slightly to herself at the way he so adamantly insisted on addressing her as Miss Garland. He always had, ever since he had joined her father's fast-growing little electronics company ten years ago as chief accountant and she had still been a skinny tomboy of barely fifteen years of age.

She, like her parents—and even her baby brother Richard—had always called him by his first name. But Lewis was a strict adherent to the old, more formal ways.

'I'm sorry, it wouldn't be respectful,' he had protested with a firm shake of his distinguished grey head when she had invited him to address her by her Christian name. 'You're the boss's daughter. I merely work here. I'd feel happier if we just left things as they are.'

And so they had—though nothing was any longer as it had been then, Olivia thought ruefully to herself as they walked briskly now along the corridor and through the swing doors into the main entrance hall. For one thing, she was no longer the boss's daughter. Garland's, as an independent company, had quite simply ceased to exist. Her father's sudden, unexpected death three years ago and her mother's hasty, ill-advised marriage to electronics mogul Roland Jordan had seen to that. Though the full extent of her mother's folly had come to light only a matter of months ago when she and her new husband had been tragically killed in a skiing accident in France.

Within months of the ill-fated union, it had been revealed, another, even less felicitous union had been arranged. And had been finalised on the very day the new Mr and Mrs Jordan had set off for the slopes of Val-d'Isère. It had both saddened and sickened Olivia to discover that, behind her own and her brother's backs, Garland's had been taken over lock, stock and barrel by Roland's mighty, grasping Jordan Electronics.

'What do you think, Miss Garland?'

As Lewis spoke, Olivia interrupted her bitter reverie to glance ceilingwards at the big, bright banner strung across the entrance hall. 'Give Us Back Our Company!' it demanded unequivocally. Then she turned to squint through the plate-glass doors at the little knots of loyal employees who were parading up and down in the chilly April sunshine bearing placards with similar slogans. She smiled with satisfaction at Lewis. 'I reckon Jordan should get the message.'

Lewis smiled back. 'I reckon he should.'

'Let's just hope it'll have the desired effect and persuade him to agree to our demands.'

'It has to.' Lewis's normally composed features creased into a frown of concern. 'If the man has any decency at all, he has to see that what we're demanding is no more than our right. *Your* right,' he amended diplomatically. 'Yours and your brother's.'

Olivia sighed. 'Above all, my brother's.' For it was Richard's future that this fight was all about. She had her own little business. Her father had set her up with the art gallery when she was twenty-one. And the plan had always been that baby brother Richard, nine years younger than herself and currently away at boarding-school, would one day take over Garland's. She smiled agreeably at Lewis. 'Let's just hope that, as you say, the man has a streak of decency. Unlike his uncle Roland.' Though, in her heart, she doubted it.

Olivia had met Roland Jordan only once and had disliked him on principle—though subsequent developments, she now felt, had proved her instant judgement right. Now, her instinctive feelings towards his heir and successor, his nephew Matthew Jordan, were equally unremittingly negative. Somehow, she strongly suspected, the man whom she was about to meet would be as unprincipled and lacking in decency as his uncle had proved to be.

Which was why she had organised this hostile little reception for him. At the very least, it would embarrass him and put him on the spot. It would be the last thing he was expecting and it was bound to unnerve him a bit.

It was just at that moment that the chanting started up outside as the groups of demonstrators came to life. 'It sounds as though they've spotted the car,' Lewis remarked in a quiet voice. He straightened his shoulders. 'This is it.'

The chanting was gathering momentum—'Jordan out! Jordan out!'—but with just the right degree of aggression, nothing unruly, as Olivia had decreed. Yet it sent a sharp chill through her bones, all the same—and a corresponding tight smile to her lips. If it had this chilling effect on her, how must it be affecting Matthew Jordan, the man at whom it was directed?

The big black company Daimler came suddenly into view through the plate-glass doors and swept to a silent halt. This was it, as Lewis had said. The moment she had so long been waiting for. Betraying her faint nervousness, Olivia unconsciously raised one hand to smooth the already immaculately smooth dark chignon at the back of her head. She had nothing to be nervous about, she told herself firmly. Lewis was there to support her. And, what was more, she had right on her side.

The man in the back seat of the Daimler didn't bother to wait for the chauffeur to come round and open up the door for him. Instead, the instant the big car drew to a halt, the passenger door opened and he stepped outside.

Olivia squinted curiously, anxious to size him up, and it crossed her mind with a flicker of annoyance that he was not at all what she had been expecting. She had envisaged some slightly stuffy-looking middle-aged executive dressed in a regulation pin-stripe suit. This man was much younger—in his middle thirties, she guessed. Tall, dark-haired and broad-shouldered—and dressed in a sharply cut navy suit that, even from this distance, she could tell bore some stylish Italian designer label.

All of that was irritating enough, but what irritated her even more was the fact that, in spite of the increased volume of chanting that went up as he hurried up the short flight of steps to the glass front doors, there was absolutely nothing in his demeanour to suggest that he was even faintly embarrassed by the demonstration. Unnerved, he most certainly was not. On the contrary, there was an expression almost of disdainful amusement on his dark-tanned features as the plate-glass doors buzzed open automatically and he came striding into the hall.

And there was something so powerful about his presence, something that commandeered the eye, that Olivia almost failed to notice the blonde girl carrying the briefcase who had emerged behind him out of the car and was scurrying behind him up the steps.

In a few short strides he had crossed the entrance hall and was standing in front of Olivia, his hand outstretched. 'Miss Garland, I presume? Matthew Jordan,' he announced.

As, briefly, they shook hands, Olivia found herself looking into a face of strong, firm lines—straight nose, square jaw and a pair of deep hazel eyes beneath straight black brows that spoke of a shrewd and ruthless intelligence. The clasp of his hand was firm and cool, discreetly authoritative. And his tanned complexion and strong, athletic build suggested a man who spent as much time engaged in outdoor, physical pursuits as he did ensconced behind a desk.

It would take a great deal more than a few chanting demonstrators to unnerve Matthew Jordan, she guessed.

But Olivia was not unnerved easily either, though a shaft of uneasiness went through her. Holding his gaze without a flicker, she gestured towards the grey-haired man at her side. 'Allow me to introduce you to Lewis Ottley who, as you know, has been running Garland's since my father died.'

The two men shook hands, then Matthew Jordan turned with a slight smile to introduce the blonde girl at his side. 'Celine Barbour, my personal secretary,' he informed them economically.

For the first time Olivia looked at the girl properly, taking in the wide, coquettish, liberally made-up eyes, the fluffy, expensively coiffed hairdo and the highly impractical and unbusinesslike cream-coloured two-piece she was wearing. And, as they exchanged greetings, for no good reason she was aware of a sharp buzz of antipathy. Celine Barbour, she sensed, was not destined to become a bosom pal.

But it was the blonde girl's boss who was once more claiming Olivia's attention as he cut in now in a sarcastic tone, 'I would suggest, Miss Garland, that you bring your protesters indoors now. I think they've adequately made their point.' Then a hint of steely amusement sparked deep in the hazel eyes as he added in blatant mock concern, 'Besides, it must be rather chilly for them out there.'

His air of easy superiority rankled. 'They're not complaining,' she shot back sharply.

'But I am.' The amusement had gone from his eyes. His tone was clipped, uncompromising. His gaze swept her suddenly flushed face as he added for good measure, 'Perhaps you would also be good enough to arrange the immediate removal of this.' He indicated with evident distaste the banner that stretched across the entrance hall. 'And I do mean *immediate*, Miss Garland.'

Almost visibly, Olivia winced. They had barely met and already the gloves were off. She had just been delivered a sharp reminder that, whether she liked it or not, Matthew Jordan was the boss around here now. But she managed to look back at him steadily and responded with almost tangible sarcasm, 'I'm sorry, I didn't realise you'd be so sensitive.'

He smiled back at her without humour. 'I would suggest there's a very great deal you don't know about me, Miss Garland. But please don't alarm yourself about my sensitivities.' He paused, his expression endorsing the harsh message in his words. The burden of over-sensitivity, Olivia could all too clearly see as with growing resentment she met his eyes, was not something that Matthew Jordan would be likely to suffer from. He underlined this observation now by adding peremptorily, 'Just make sure that this eyesore is removed and that ridiculous mob dispersed. Before I leave,' he emphasised.

'I'll see to it, Mr Jordan.' It was Lewis who cut in now, his tone conciliatory as he threw Olivia a soothing look. And he was right, she thought, cursing herself for her sharp, quick tongue that had so far only succeeded in further antagonising the man she desperately needed to reach an agreement with. Her roughshod tactics had done more harm than good. And she felt a surge of gratitude for Lewis's timely subtlety as he made a discreet signal to the watching receptionist before continuing, 'I suggest we adjourn for our meeting now.' Then he turned and led the way through the swing doors and along the corridor to the boardroom at the end. 'This way, Mr Jordan.'

They took their places round the polished oval mahogany table where notepads and pencils, water jugs and glasses had already been laid out. Matthew Jordan at the head, with his secretary placed decoratively on his right. On his left, Olivia, and next to her, a little further down the table, Lewis, her essential ally.

There was a stiff, strained silence as the blonde Celine took some papers from the black leather briefcase and slid them across the table towards her boss. Inwardly, Olivia made a face. So he had come prepared for battle, too—though he didn't even glance at the papers as he leaned forward, his elbows on the table, and idly picked up the yellow pencil that lay on the notepad in front of him.

He had particularly well-shaped hands, Olivia couldn't help but notice. Long-fingered, strong-looking and unadorned with rings, the tan of his skin contrasting sharply with the immaculate white cuffs of the shirt he wore. Clever, manipulative hands, she found herself thinking with mounting disapproval, that somehow per-fectly complemented the clever, manipulative gleam in his eyes.

He came straight to the point, his gaze fixed on Olivia as he spoke. 'We're here to discuss the recent merger between Garland's and Jordan Electronics. Unfortunately, Miss Garland appears to be of the opinion that there are still a few wrinkles to be ironed out.'

She held his eyes, irritated by his offhand tone of voice. 'A few wrinkles is not how I would describe the problems, Mr Jordan. I would say they were much more fundamental than that. I happen to be contesting the very validity of the merger.'

'I thought you'd already done that. And lost,' he added pointedly, a superior smile curling round his lips.

Olivia glared at him. 'I'm aware of that,' she assured him cuttingly. How could she be anything else after three months of legal wrangling that had left her spiritually exhausted and severely out of pocket? The courts had come down unequivocally on the side of Jordan's. The merger was perfectly legally valid. 'What I'm contesting now,' she bit at him between clenched teeth, 'is its moral validity.'

Matthew Jordan seemed to find that amusing. He smiled briefly, revealing perfect white teeth. 'Moral validity?' he repeated, watching her. 'I thought this was to be a business discussion. I had no idea that you intended extending the proceedings into the realms of moral philosophy.'

'Not your strong point, I've no doubt.' Then she added recklessly, 'Straightforward theft appears to be more in line with the Jordan family's repertoire.'

As the amusement drained abruptly from his face, to be replaced with an expression like splintered glass, Olivia silently cursed herself for having gone too far again. Her accusation was undoubtedly true, but in the circumstances she might have been wiser to couch it in somewhat more diplomatic terms. She dropped her gaze awkwardly, as he ground back angrily at her; 'Perhaps, Miss Garland, you would care to elaborate on that last remark?'

As she fumbled for words, a reluctant apology on her lips, Lewis came to the rescue again. 'I fear Miss Garland is expressing herself badly. She is, quite understandably, deeply distressed by the events of the past few months. The death of her mother—a terrible blow.' He spoke quietly, urging forbearance, all the while fiddling self-consciously with the heavy gold signet ring he wore on the middle finger of his right hand. 'And then this totally expected development regarding the take-over of her family's firm——'

'*Merger*. Not takeover,' Matthew Jordan quickly corrected him, though his expression had softened a bit. He sat back in his seat and let his eyes travel back to Olivia. 'I realise that your mother's death must have been a blow for you—and I also realise that the merger must have come as something of a surprise.' He paused for a moment and narrowed his eyes. 'It also came as a surprise to me.'

Somehow Olivia doubted that, but she carefully bit the observation back. Instead she told him in an even tone, deliberately using the term he had rejected, 'Your uncle evidently believed that the takeover would be useful to Jordan's. The area in which Garland's specialises—and holds a con-siderable share of the European market—is an area in which Jordan's has been seeking a foothold for some time, I understand.' She reeled off to perfec-tion a string of statistics to back up her point, and was aware of Lewis nodding his approval at her side. Encouraged, she continued, 'The reasons why your uncle wished to get his hands on my mother's company are fairly self-evident. Since my mother received not one penny in compensation, the reasons why she chose to part with it are open to interpretation . . .'

As she paused, her expression censorious, he

raised a dark, inquisitive eyebrow. 'And your interpretation, I presume, is that she was somehow tricked? That my uncle used some dishonest ploy in order to steal her company from her . . .?'

'Precisely.' The blue eyes were hard. 'Perhaps it was specifically for that reason that he married her.'

Matthew Jordan shrugged broad shoulders and straightened the cerise silk tie at his throat. 'I somehow doubt it,' he said, and smiled that infuriatingly superior smile. 'Garland's may have been a useful acquisition, but it's not exactly ICI, after all.'

Olivia tightened her lips defensively, resenting the deliberately belittling remark. 'Nevertheless,' she pointed out acidly, 'I notice you're not in any particular hurry to give it back.'

'I have, however, agreed to pay a considerable financial remuneration.'

'That's not what I want. It was my father's wish that Garland's should be passed on to my brother. And it is likewise my own wish and that of my brother.'

Matthew Jordan sat forward in his seat again, the shrewd eyes scrutinising her face, long fingers toying idly with the yellow pencil. 'As an alternative, I have offered your brother a share in Jordan's commensurate with the stake of Garland's, a guaranteed executive position with the company when he graduates from college and a seat on the board when he reaches twenty-five. I would suggest that in terms of compensation either offer would be considered more than generous.'

Olivia regarded him stubbornly. There was no way he was going to sweet-talk her round. 'I repeat, that's not what we want, Mr Jordan. We want our company back.'

He leaned back in his seat again, the pencil delicately poised between the tips of the strong, tanned index fingers, and met her gaze with easy, unruffled self-assurance. 'In that case, I'm afraid I can't help you,' he said.

'Can't or won't?' There was ice in her voice.

'Can't, Miss Garland, alas. Even if I wanted to, such a move is quite beyond my powers.'

Olivia looked back at him with open scepticism in her eyes. 'Forgive me if I find that just a little difficult to believe.' She happened to know that, with the death of his uncle, he had acquired an overwhelming majority on the board of Jordan's. According to Lewis's meticulous research, he virtually ran the huge company single-handed. His claim was simply one more example of the Jordan family's predisposition towards chicanery and lies. 'Don't try to tell me that such a simple matter as signing a few papers would be beyond your capabilities?'

'Beyond my capabilities, no.' A cruelly sardonic smile touched his lips. 'But, I'm afraid, quite beyond my jurisdiction.'

'How come?'

'How come?' He repeated the bald enquiry with another mocking little smile, then paused for a moment before answering to deliberately clear his throat. Instantly the blonde Celine, who had sat silent but attentive so far, reached for the nearest water jug to fill her boss's empty glass and, with a geisha-like smile, offered it to him. With the barest of acknowledgements, Matthew Jordan accepted the glass and drank.

Olivia observed the little ceremony with mixed discomfort and distaste, but without any degree of real surprise. She had already judged the blonde girl as belonging to that type of female who believe it is their place to perform services for men. Involuntarily she felt a stab of pain. She knew the type well. Her own mother had been one. With ever-strengthening disapproval, she raised her eyes to Matthew Jordan. It was equally easy to recognise in him a man who accepted—even demanded—such grovelling gestures as his right. That type was painfully close to home as well.

She waited until he had finished drinking and laid the half-empty glass aside. 'Well? You haven't answered my question,' she said.

'I'm about to, Miss Garland, if you'll just give me the chance.' He leaned back casually in his seat and began toying with the yellow pencil again. 'Though I'm afraid you won't find much comfort in what I have to say.'

Olivia regarded him flatly and said nothing. Somehow she was afraid of that, too.

He began, the hazel eyes beneath the straight black brows watching her closely as he spoke, 'My great-uncle Julius, who founded Jordan's, was a very family-orientated man. It was always his strongest desire that the company should remain within the family.'

He paused, as though to ensure maximum

impact for what was coming next—and smiled a tantalising smile, evidently enjoying his audience's unease. 'To that end,' he continued, 'he had inserted in the company's charter a clause which prohibits any part of the company passing into the hands of anyone who is not a family member.' He tossed the yellow pencil casually to one side and spelled out what Olivia had already deduced for herself. 'Since Garland's is now an integral part of Jordan Electronics, I'm afraid that unfortunate clause applies. As I already told you, even if it were my wish, it is quite outside my jurisdiction to return Garland's to you.'

Olivia was staring at him, open-mouthed. 'But that's preposterous!' she began.

Then she glanced at Lewis for support and nodded vigorously in agreement as the wily accountant proposed, 'Surely, Mr Jordan, a way can be found round such a clause? There must be some legal loophole that would apply in these exceptional circumstances.' He twisted the ring on his middle finger as he smiled across the table at Matthew Jordan. 'If you were agreeable, couldn't our lawyers——?'

'I'm afraid not, Mr Ottley,' Matthew Jordan cut in rudely. 'The clause is watertight. I can assure you now that you would be wasting your time if you were to endeavour to find a way around it.'

Momentarily, Lewis fell silent, but Olivia's brain was working overtime. 'Our mother was married to your uncle,' she challenged. 'Doesn't that qualify my brother and me as family under the clause?'

He shook his dark head in mock regret. 'Alas,

Miss Garland, I'm afraid it doesn't. The clause was highly specific in its definition of family. Our rather tenuous relationship wouldn't legally qualify.' A taunting smile crossed the dark-tanned face. 'The old man left nothing to chance. I suppose you could say that when he set up Jordan's he was doing more than merely founding a business. It was his intention, in a way, to establish a family——'

'Dynasty,' Olivia finished for him in her most cutting voice. Megalomania and self-importance were evidently in his genes. Though, privately, she was wishing that her own father had had the foresight to make similar arrangements himself. It looked as if the business he had founded for his heirs had passed forever out of Garland hands. She felt a sudden plummet of despair. She had been so certain that with a bit of hard bargaining face to face she would be able to win her case. Now she felt as though an impenetrable brick wall had suddenly sprung up in front of her.

She stared at Matthew Jordan, hating him, as without a gram of sympathy or regret in his voice he told her, 'So you see, my hands are tied.'

'How convenient!' she shot back contemptuously. It probably suited him very well.

Unperturbed, he put to her, 'You may take your time in deciding which of my two options you prefer to accept. I trust you will wish to discuss the matter with your brother before coming to a decision.'

'I have no need to discuss the matter with Richard. I know he wants his company back.'

With a weary gesture, he shook his head. 'I've

already explained to you why that's not possible. Your options are those I've already spelled out—unless you have any other suggestions . . .?'

Olivia had none—for the moment. Though she wasn't about to give up yet. There had to be some way out of this impasse. 'I'm going to go on fighting you.'

He turned away indifferently. 'That's entirely up to you, Miss Garland. You're perfectly free to waste your time if that's what you wish to do. In the meantime——' for the first time, he glanced down at the papers his secretary had laid in front of him, 'I've arranged for one of my top men to move in as deputy director. For the next few months he'll be working alongside you, Mr Ottley,' he said, addressing the grey-haired man. 'Getting to know the company, learning the ropes.'

Olivia felt herself stiffen with indignation. That sounded ominously like a threat to the position of her staunchest ally. Why would he appoint a deputy unless he intended that deputy to take over? 'I thought you promised there'd be no staff changes when you took over the company?' she challenged, an edge to her voice.

'Have I made any?' he enquired rhetorically. 'This, for the moment, is a straightforward addition.' With smooth insincerity, he addressed himself to Lewis. 'I'm sure Mr Ottley has no objections to having someone to share the burdens of leadership with him for a while?'

'Of course not.' Though Lewis appeared outwardly calm, Olivia could sense his inner dismay. And she felt for him. Over the years since her father had died, he had done an excellent job of keeping the company going. He didn't deserve to be treated like this.

But even as she opened her mouth to protest on his behalf, Matthew Jordan was pushing the file of papers across the table towards him. 'His name's McKay. This is a copy of his CV. You can acquaint yourself with his particulars before he arrives next week.' Then he glanced quickly at the pale gold watch at his wrist. 'My secretary has need of the use of a phone in private for a couple of minutes. Perhaps——'

'She can use the one in my office.' Already Lewis was rising to his feet. No doubt, thought Olivia with sympathy, he was glad of the opportunity to escape. He gathered up the odious papers. 'Allow me to accompany you.'

As the blonde Celine rose sinuously from her seat and followed Lewis to the door, her boss instructed, 'Once you're finished, just wait in the car. I'll be out in a couple of minutes.'

The girl smiled sweetly, 'Very well, Mr Jordan,' and Olivia scoffed inwardly to herself. 'Mr Jordan' indeed! I'll bet it's 'Matthew' in private! Somehow she sensed that carrying his briefcase and thoughtfully pouring him glasses of water were not the only services the delectable Celine performed for her boss.

As the door closed and they were left alone, Matthew Jordan turned to her. 'Perhaps now, Miss Garland, you wouldn't mind just quickly showing me round the works?'

'Me?' She raised a sarcastic eyebrow at him.

'Why ask me? I have nothing to do with Garland's any more—as you've been at great pains all afternoon to point out. I think it would be more fitting if Mr Ottley or one of the other senior members of staff were to do the honours.'

She stood up, intending to cross to the phone. But before she was even half-way there, he had risen too and stepped in front of her. 'That won't be necessary, Miss Garland. As much as I hate to incommode you, I'm sure your knowledge of the place, for the moment, will suffice.'

He was standing so close that she took a step back, overwhelmed by the raw male power of him. As he took a step forward, closing the gap, she could feel his warmth, his clean, masculine scent. She felt suddenly threatened, deeply confused; her hand fluttered protectively to her high-necked blouse. Her mouth felt dry. She cleared her throat. 'Very well,' she croaked.

Her heart was still hammering furiously as she turned abruptly and led him through the door, then along another corridor to the part of the building where the design and assembly work was done. And what infuriated her even more than her own pathetic, schoolgirlish response was the fact that she knew he was perfectly aware of the total confusion he had caused in her. And that the spectacle of her embarrassed floundering had quite evidently appealed to his warped sense of humour.

An amused gleam shone in the bright hazel eyes as he stepped ahead of her into the busy assembly area and took a look around. 'So this is it?' He did not sound impressed.

'Yes, Mr Jordan, this is it.' Olivia threw him a shrewd look. 'A modest establishment by your standards, I'm sure. Hardly worth hanging on to, really.'

He regarded her from top to toe, and there was an insinuatingly ambiguous note in his voice as he told her, 'Tut, tut, Miss Garland. Don't sell yourself short. All it needs is a few months in the right hands to make the most of its potential.'

As he started to make his own way round, Olivia followed silently, hating the calm way he took control. Hating, too, the easy manner in which he introduced himself and exchanged pleasantries with various members of the workforce as he paused here and there along the way. He was nothing but a calculating bastard, just like his uncle!

And he was taking his time, she observed, in spite of his earlier assurance that this would just be a very brief tour. She had a sudden flash of the passive Celine sitting outside in the car, waiting patiently for him. She was no doubt used to this sort of thing. And also, no doubt, never complained. A doormat, custom-made for an arrogant male chauvinist like Matthew Jordan.

Eventually he told her, 'OK, I've seen enough,' and with a heartfelt sense of relief Olivia started to accompany him back along the corridor towards the swing doors that led out into the entrance hall. Though he walked quickly, she forced herself to keep pace with him, and they were abreast as they came together to the set of double swing doors.

Virtually simultaneously, they reached out to push the doors wide, and for one brief but breathtaking moment their two hands collided.

As warm flesh brushed against warm flesh, Olivia snatched her hand away, feeling almost as though she had been burned. And she was excruciatingly aware of the sudden hot colour that flooded her face as Matthew Jordan deliberately held her eyes for a moment before gallantly stepping aside. 'After you, Miss Garland. Ladies first.'

Stiffly, she manoeuvred past him out into the entrance hall, registering with mingled relief and regret that the welcoming banner had been taken down while, outside, only the Daimler waited, with no sign of the demonstrators or their placards. It irked her that he should have had his way, but she was grateful to be spared any further confrontation. The only thing she wanted now was to see him climb into the big black car and, she hoped, never set eyes on him again.

Politely she accompanied him to the plate-glass doors. 'I hope you have a pleasant trip home.' And a speedy one, she added to herself.

He smiled. 'Oh, I won't be going back south just yet. I'll be around until tomorrow.' His smile widened as hers wavered at this news. 'If you should wish to get in touch with me, I'm staying at the Royal.'

Thanks for the warning, Olivia thought—and waited impatiently for him to go.

But again he was taking his time. 'Likewise, if some fresh solution occurs to me, I might give you a call. Don't worry,' he enjoined perversely as she opened her mouth to protest, 'I already have your home number on file.'

Did he, indeed? A disquieting thought.

'You will be spending the evening at home, I take it?

'I may be.' She eyed him indignantly, taking exception to the casual insult implicit in his assumption. Then she added in a studiedly offhand tone, 'Sydney and I will probably be having a quiet evening in for a change.'

'Sydney?' One dark eyebrow lifted in undisguised surprise. But, to her immense relief, he did not pursue the subject. Instead he smiled and held out his hand. 'It's been a pleasure meeting you.'

There was no way she would perjure herself by returning the fraudulent compliment. With stiff reluctance, she extended her own hand. 'Goodbye, Mr Jordan,' she replied.

Perhaps if Olivia had been feeling a bit less agitated, she might have anticipated his next move. As it was, what happened next took her totally by surprise.

Graciously, Matthew Jordan took her hand and, just for a moment, held her eyes. Then, before she realised what was happening, he bent towards her and raised the back of her hand to his lips—a kiss that scorched like molten fire against her unsuspecting flesh.

'Not goodbye, Miss Garland,' he told her, straightening. 'Merely *au revoir*.'

Then, leaving her standing apopleptic with rage, he turned and walked calmly out through the doors.

CHAPTER TWO

THE FIRST thing Olivia did that evening when she got home was take the phone off the hook.

Matthew Jordan's little threat to give her a call if some new solution came to mind had undoubtedly been made in jest. For one thing, he had all but convinced her that no possible solutions existed, other than those he had already proposed. For another, right now his mind was probably engaged in rather more frivolous pursuits. In the shape of the fair Celine. Like the good little geisha that she was, she would be helping her master to unwind.

But with a man like Matthew Jordan one could never be entirely sure. Hence the disconnected phone. Somehow Olivia sensed he was just the type who would take a devilish delight in deliberately disrupting her peace and quiet.

As she kicked off her shoes, Sydney was lying curled up on the sofa. She bent to give his ear an affectionate tug. 'So it's just you and me, as usual,' she said with a slight smile to herself as the big ginger cat yawned lazily, then stretched and went back to sleep.

Suddenly her lips pursed as she remembered the look of surprise on Matthew Jordan's face when she had casually dropped in Sydney's name. Even now she wasn't quite sure why she'd done it. Nor why his reaction had irked her so.

She went through to the bedroom and quickly undressed. Then, in the adjoining bathroom, she glanced at her reflection in the mirror as she pulled on a shower cap and switched on the shower. Beneath the sober, businesslike suit and the plain, restricting blouse, her slim figure was surprisingly curvy, with firm, high breasts, a tiny waist and legs that were long and shapely and slender.

Outwardly, she might not be the ultra-feminine, ego-stroking type of female that men like Matthew Jordan preferred, but she was indisputably all woman underneath. But a woman on her own terms, not on the terms of some egocentric man who would take over her life and use her, then scorn her when he had tired of her.

That was the fate she had seen fall to her mother as the wife of an ambitious and insensitive man whose only true concerns had ever been himself and his precious career. Throughout her childhood Olivia had watched the ritual humiliation of her mother, conveniently honoured with the role of wife for the occasional public appearance, neglected and treated with studied contempt for the remainder of the time. And the agony that, at times, she had seen staring out of her mother's eyes was burned like a brand across her brain.

At a very young age Olivia had made a vow that no man would ever get close enough to inflict such pain and humiliation on her. Hence the outward shell of independence and untouchability that she had cultivated to protect herself. For, deep in her soul, she knew—and feared—her own immense vulnerability.

With a sigh, she stepped under the shower and allowed the warm, spiky jets of water to sluice away the day's aggravations. Which today, she had to confess, had been considerably more aggravating than usual. Matthew Jordan had succeeded in getting her back up in a way that very few people did.

Quickly she rubbed herself dry with one of the big pink stripey towels, then smoothed in body lotion from head to toe before padding back into the bedroom and slipping on a loose burgundy caftan—her customary attire for relaxing at home. Next she unpinned the neat, tight chignon, letting her long dark hair fall loose to her shoulders, then applied a couple of vigorous strokes of her hairbrush before stuffing her feet into gold leather mules and returning to the living-room.

Gratefully she slumped down on the sofa beside Sydney, feeling the tension in her start to ebb away as she gently stroked the thick ginger fur, smiling contentedly to herself as the cat stretched languorously and purred. She reached for the TV remote control. She'd watch her favourite chat show for half an hour, then stick a TV dinner in the microwave. No cooking tonight. Just a lazy, relaxing evening in front of the box. She could start reconsidering her strategy regarding Richard and his future tomorrow, after a good night's sleep.

But such an agreeable itinerary was destined to fall foul of fate. She had just poured herself a small glass of wine and was sinking back against the sofa cushions when, to her dismay, the doorbell rang.

Damn. Who could that be? Olivia laid down her drink on the coffee-table and hurried reluctantly out into the hall. It was rare for anyone to turn up at her flat at this time of the evening unannounced. Though it was probably just some neighbour collecting for charity, she assured herself as she opened up the door.

It was no neighbour. And it was most certainly no charity. Dismay turned to abject horror as her eyes met those of the tall, dark figure standing in the outer hallway.

'Good evening, Miss Garland,' he intoned with a smile.

Olivia glared up at him, wishing with a vengeance that she'd had the foresight to ignore the bell. Without returning his greeting, she demanded rudely, 'What do you think you're doing here?'

He was wearing a different suit from the one he had worn that afternoon—mid-grey, slightly less formal, with a light blue shirt and royal blue tie. With total poise, he leaned in the doorway and surveyed her unhurriedly up and down, his dark hair gleaming in the bright hall lights, an insolent smile in the deep hazel eyes. 'It's your lucky night, Miss Garland,' he told her. 'I've come to take you out to dinner.'

What a preposterous idea! Olivia's eyes narrowed as she told him curtly, 'Then I'm afraid you've wasted your time. I already have other plans for dinner.'

'With Sydney?' A mocking smile curled round Matthew Jordan's lips. 'Surely he could spare you for just one night?'

Olivia straightened defensively. Already he was getting her back up again. 'My plans are really none of your business. I've already told you, you've wasted your time.' And, with a flourish, she made to close the door.

'Hold on just a minute, Miss Garland. Not quite so fast!' With an almost imperceptible movement he stepped forward and jammed his foot in the door. Then, without a glimmer of a smile, he went on to inform her, 'I have a proposition I think you might be interested to hear.'

Olivia stopped short and stared suspiciously at him. 'What proposition?' she wanted to know.

The slow, taunting smile returned to his lips. 'The proposition I intend discussing over our little business dinner. Rest assured,' he added with a twist, 'my invitation is strictly in the interests of business, not pleasure. Surely you don't think I'd give up my evening just to enjoy your gracious company?' Then, as she continued to hesitate, he enquired, 'Are you going to invite me in, or must we conduct this conversation on the doorstep, Miss Garland?'

Stiffly, reluctantly, Olivia stood aside and watched with fierce irritation as he strode past her into the drawing-room.

He glanced round. 'Very nice.' Then he continued as she stood poker-faced in the doorway watching him, 'I tried to phone you a couple of times, but your line was constantly engaged.' He tossed an amused look at the little table where the phone sat, receiver detached. 'Now I understand why.'

Inwardly, Olivia cursed herself. If she hadn't taken the phone off the hook to pre-empt his threatened call, she would have been spared the infinitely more distasteful alternative of having him turn up in the flesh at her front door. At least, on the phone, she could have put him off by protesting some prior engagement. In person, he would not be quite so easy to dispose of—a supposition to which he gave instant substance by seating himself comfortably in one of her chintz chairs.

As Olivia came to stand before him in the centre of the room, he nodded in the direction of the dozing ginger cat. 'So that's Sydney,' he observed with one of his amused, superior smiles.

Olivia coloured slightly and glared at him in silence with every ounce of loathing that she felt.

'Somehow I suspected he'd turn out to be a cat.' His smile curled wickedly at the corners. 'Or perhaps a budgerigar.' Slowly he looked her up and down. 'One thing I knew for certain was that he wouldn't be a man.'

'Did you?' Her tone was flat. She resisted the temptation to ask him why.

But he went on to tell her anyway. 'A man can tell such things about a woman, you know. You're definitely the chaste and spinsterish type.'

Abruptly Olivia dropped her eyes, momentarily caught off balance by his direct, unchivalrous remark. Though he had definitely been right about one thing, at least. She was nothing if not chaste. But she had never thought of herself as spinsterish —career-minded, perhaps—and she wasn't quite sure if she cared for the tag. Still, she swiftly reminded herself, Matthew Jordan's evaluation of her was really the last thing she cared about. She glanced up and threw him a glacial look. 'You said you had some kind of proposition. Perhaps you could just get on and tell me what it is.'

He reached for one of the magazines that lay strewn on the top of the coffee-table and leafed through it unhurriedly. 'I've already told you—we'll discuss it over dinner.'

'And I've already told you that I have no intention of having dinner with you.' She stepped forward, confronting him, and folded her arms across her chest. 'If you have something to say, you can say it here. And then, once you've said it, you can go.'

He tossed the magazine aside and gave her a long, slow, lingering look. His tone when he spoke was that of a long-suffering parent addressing a particularly tiresome child. 'Look, my dear Miss Garland,' he told her, 'I happen to be very tired. I've had a long day and I haven't eaten properly since breakfast-time. With or without you, I'm going to have dinner. If you want to hear my proposition, fine. Come along. I can assure you,' he added on a sarcastic note, 'I'm not planning to try and seduce you over the *soufflé surprise.*'

He raised one straight black eyebrow and concluded, 'It's up to you. Make up your mind. If you'd rather stay at home with Sydney, we can just forget the whole thing.'

He meant it. Beneath that sometimes supercilious façade lurked an unbending will. And it would be foolish, Olivia knew, out of personal dislike to pass up the opportunity of hearing what he had to say. It could be important. It was her responsibility to Richard to hear his proposition out.

'Well?' He was waiting, yet poised as though ready to get up and go.

'OK, I'll go and get dressed.' She dropped her arms in gracious defeat and started to move off in the direction of her room.

'As quick as you can. I'm hungry, remember. And there's a taxi waiting downstairs with its meter running.' He watched her go with an amused, triumphant smile. Then he added, as he picked up the magazine again and started flicking through it, 'And leave your hair down, the way it is. I prefer it like that.'

Did he, indeed? The wretched cheek of the man! As Olivia hurried through to her room, carefully locking the door before slipping off her caftan and rummaging in the cupboard for something suitable to wear, she could feel unbridled anger bubbling inside. Matthew Jordan was an insufferable, opinionated, overbearing bully, the type of man she would run a mile to avoid. An evening in his company had about as much appeal as a kick in the head!

She picked out a favourite long-sleeved black dress whose simplicity belied its elegant cut—wide-shouldered, high-necked, the hem skimming her shapely knees. Then she pulled on a pair of sheer black tights, slipped her feet into plain black courts and regarded her reflection in the mirror. A heavy gold necklace at her throat with matching earrings in her ears, and she was almost ready to appear.

Almost. With defiant pleasure she deftly twisted her long dark hair to the back of her head and secured it in a neat chignon. So he preferred it loose, did he? The desert would blossom with waterlilies before she adjusted her appearance to please him!

As she walked back into the drawing-room, her black cashmere cape draped softly round her shoulders, Matthew Jordan was already on his feet. He gave her a scrutinising look, irritating her and making her blush. 'A bit severe, but it'll do,' he said.

He hadn't been joking about the taxi that was waiting downstairs, its meter clocking up the pounds. And, as she climbed in, the spiteful thought crossed Olivia's mind that she should have taken her time about dressing. Not that a few pounds meant anything to Matthew Jordan, she reminded herself bitterly as he instructed the driver to take them to the most expensive French restaurant in town. Not a few pounds. Not a few hundred pounds. Not even a few thousand pounds, most probably. Which simply made it all the more galling that he and his family had stolen her brother's precious inheritance.

The waiter took her cape with a smile. 'Good evening, Miss Garland. Good evening, sir.' Then he seated them at one of the better tables, in a discreet corner with a view out over the restaurant. As he handed them a pair of enormous menus—no prices on hers, she noted—Matthew Jordan regarded her with amusement across the table.

'Evidently one of your regular stamping grounds. When you're not dining with Sydney, you come here, do you?'

Olivia threw him a deliberately false smile as she

laid her napkin across her lap. 'I occasionally come here for lunch,' she told him. 'When I have clients to entertain.'

'Your clients. Of course.' He smiled again, she thought a trifle patronisingly. 'The little art gallery you run. It's quite a success, I understand.'

Did he? Matthew Jordan, it appeared, knew a great deal more about her affairs than she would have wished. She looked back at him coldly. 'It does quite well, thank you,' she confirmed.

'You run it alone?'

'I have an assistant.' An invaluable one. Without the level-headed Jeffrey Parker's input—especially on the accounting side—The Gallery, as her little establishment was called, would never have become the success it was.

Matthew Jordan was leaning back in his chair, watching her over the top of his menu with those deep hazel eyes. 'I had a look at some of the paintings in your flat while you were getting ready,' he told her. 'I have to admit you have good taste.'

That was definitely patronising! Olivia laid down her menu and fixed him with a stony stare. 'I'm honoured by the compliment,' she told him with heavy irony.

He was undeterred. 'I mean it. You obviously possess a considerable artistic eye.'

Olivia sniffed. 'I'm a businesswoman, not an artist, Mr Jordan. I have an instinct for a marketable commodity. I know what sells. That's all there is to it.'

'Yet you ended up selling paintings, not computers.' He probed her with a look. 'I think that suggests an artistic bent.'

'Think what you will. Business is business.' The last thing she was going to allow was that he lead her into a discussion of her paintings. Thanks to years of practice with her father, she had long ago learnt the subtle techniques of fending off patronising remarks, but her 'artistic bent', as he had called it, was still terrain too close to her heart to allow a man like Matthew Jordan to invade. Fending him off, she emphasised, 'Selling paintings is a business, just like any other.'

A faint smile flickered at the corner of his lips. He paused for a moment, then asked, 'So tell me, how long have you been running this business of yours?'

'Almost four years. My father bought it for me just before he died.' After a tooth-and-nail fight, she might have added. 'I could have gone into Garland's, of course, but I preferred the prospect of an independent career, one that I could control myself.' Working alongside her father would have been impossible. She could never have stood for his tempers and his bullying, the way the rest of the workforce had to do. But she kept this to herself as well. Such a stance would find little sympathy with Jordan, every inch the bullying autocrat himself. Instead she added, 'Besides, my brother has been passionately interested in computers ever since he was a little kid. It made sense that, one day, Garland's would be his.' She paused, her blue eyes narrowing now as she put to him, 'Which brings us neatly to the point we came here to discuss. This proposition of yours.' She leaned across the table and demanded boldly, 'Perhaps you'd like to spell it out?'

'First things first.' As the waiter chose that very moment to arrive soundlessly at their table, she could sense Matthew Jordan's evident delight at this opportunity to thwart her again. 'Let's order first, shall we?' he suggested with a wicked gleam in his eye. 'I hate talking business on an empty stomach.'

They ordered *fruits de mer* as their starter, Olivia plumping for *poulet* to follow, Matthew Jordan selecting the chef's special steak. And to accompany it all he chose a bottle of claret—of a particularly desirable vintage, judging by the wine waiter's nod of approval.

But the instant they were left alone again Olivia returned to press her point. 'Your proposition, Mr Jordan. I want to hear it.'

Matthew Jordan sat back slightly in his seat and ran long, tanned fingers across his short, dark hair. The broad, smooth brow furrowed slightly as he looked across at her and the deep voice was low and sincere as he began to explain, 'To be perfectly honest, I have no idea what private agreement might have existed between your mother and my uncle when he took over Garland's—nor even what the reasons for the merger might have been. Though I've tried, I've been unable to track down any records of the deal.' He shrugged. 'I can't understand why.'

'I'll tell you why. Because it was theft. One doesn't normally keep records of one's crimes.'

'There's one thing I do know,' he continued, his

voice never faltering, ignoring her gibe, 'and that is that my uncle was an honest man. It would never have been his intention to short-change your mother or her family—in any way. That's why I've already offered you what I consider to be generous compensation.'

Olivia leaned her elbows on the table, her tone derisive as she told him, 'Let me tell you something, Mr Jordan. I met your uncle Roland once. He was one of those charming, honey-tongued men who find it all too easy to manipulate women . . .'

She fixed him with a look of censure, resisting the urge to observe aloud that he had evidently inherited those particular attributes of his uncle's along with all the Jordan millions—attributes to which she personally was happily immune. Instead she told him bluntly, 'My mother, unfortunately, was one of those women who are easily led. She could be talked into almost anything, especially by a man.' She fixed him with another harsh look. 'But I'm not my mother, Mr Jordan. That's why I reject your so-called generous compensation. Garland's is worth a great deal more than a few paltry shares in Jordan Electronics!'

For a moment he did not look at her, just toyed idly with his knife, the tan of his fingers dark against the pale linen tablecloth. Then slowly, deliberately, he raised his eyes. 'To call the shares I've offered paltry is to somewhat overstate your case. They're worth considerably more than Garland's is ever likely to be. However,' he hurried on before she could interrupt, 'I can see that owning shares in a larger company over which one has no real control is not quite the same as running a company of one's own.' He paused significantly. 'Hence this new proposition of mine.'

There was something about the expression in his eyes that made Olivia hold her breath. Suddenly she had the feeling that they might be on the brink of something crucial. Silently she put up a prayer. Was it possible, after all, that he had found a way round that ridiculous clause?

She swallowed. 'Namely?'

He straightened. 'Namely this.' But he seemed to hesitate a moment before continuing, 'In addition to my previous offer of shares in Jordan's and a guaranteed job, I'm also prepared to offer your brother—after an initial period of training—nominal control of Garland's. He'll be free to run it more or less as though it were his own.'

'Nominal control of Garland's!' Hope turned to cold disappointment in her breast. She had totally misread that look in his eyes. 'I'm sorry, I can't accept that,' she said.

He glanced away. 'It's the best I can do.'

'Well, it's not good enough. We want our company back.'

He threw her a cold look. 'I've already explained to you the reason why that can't be done. Great-Uncle Julius's clause is foolproof.' He smiled. 'He was a clever man.'

Bitterly, Olivia sat silent as the waiter arrived with the claret. And through eyes clouded with resentment and anger she watched as Matthew Jordan tasted the wine—swirling it expertly in his glass, then raising it briefly to his nostrils before taking a sip. They were all so damned clever, these Jordans. Clever and slippery and devious. How could her mother have been so gullible as to become involved with any of them?

As the wine was approved and the hors-d'oeuvres arrived, they were left alone again. Olivia stared without appetite at the seafood on her plate. She had been stupid to come. She might have known it would be a waste of time.

Matthew Jordan was half-way through his starter. He paused to glance across at her. 'Once you've had a chance to think properly about my offer, I'm sure you'll realise it's more than fair.'

'Fair!' She reached for her wine and dismissed the notion in one contemptuous syllable. The Jordan view of fairness and her own quite clearly did not coincide.

'Talk it over with your brother and see what he thinks of it. Or I'll have a chat with him, if you'd prefer.' As she drank, ignoring him, he added in a reasonable tone, 'Perhaps he has some ideas of his own that we might be able to include in the deal.'

In the deal! The cool, indifferent phrase summed up his attitude to a T! Olivia felt herself go stiff, her fingers tightening around the stem of her glass so fiercely that it very nearly snapped in two. All the anger and frustration bubbling inside her was suddenly threatening to explode. She laid down the glass carefully and glared across the table at him.

'In spite of what you seem to believe, Mr Jordan, this isn't some business deal we're talking about here. What we're talking about is my brother's future that's been stolen from him! And if you think

I'm just going to stand back passively and let that happen, then I'm afraid you couldn't be more mistaken!' She paused for a moment to gulp in breath. 'My brother and I—not to mention my mother—have already suffered enough because of Garland's. All our lives we took second place to the company. The only thing that made that tolerable— at least to my mother and me—was knowing that one day Richard would benefit.'

She glanced away to hide her hurt and anger. 'And he would have done if she hadn't had the misfortune to meet and marry your uncle. Heaven knows, after what she'd been through with my father, I would have thought she'd have had more sense.' She paused abruptly and bit her lip, slightly regretting the indiscreet slip. Then she hurried on, 'But I don't suppose anyone could have guessed she'd be even unluckier the second time. At least my father left her with something. All your uncle did was take it away!'

As she came to the end of her verbal fusillade, Olivia was literally shaking with emotion. She removed her hands from the tabletop and laid them in her lap, out of sight. Then she took a deep breath and lowered her head, acutely conscious of his gaze on her face.

For a long moment neither of them spoke, and the silence was deafening. Then Matthew Jordan said, very quietly, 'I get the impression you didn't think much of your father.'

A twinge of guilt went through her at his words. Had she really revealed so much? Carefully, not looking at him, she answered, 'As a businessman, I admired him greatly.' She had learned everything she knew about the business world from him. Just as she had also learned how cruel and uncaring a human heart can be. His bad-tempered bullying and vicious tongue had terrified her as child. But, with the passing of the years, terror had evolved into pure, cold contempt. She looked across at Matthew Jordan. 'I didn't admire him as a man.'

'But you were close to your mother?'

'As close as a daughter can be.' Hadn't she been much more than a daughter? Her mother's ally, comforter and friend. Resentfully she met the dark eyes. 'That is, of course, until she married your uncle. We were never quite so close after that.'

The dark brows knitted. 'Why?' he asked.

'Why?' Olivia laughed a mocking laugh. 'Because I was against the marriage from the start. To have the good fortune to escape from the clutches of one selfish and domineering man only to run straight into the arms of another struck me as masochism bordering on madness.' She paused for a moment to reflect. 'But alas, my mother was the type of woman who finds it hard to live without a man.'

Something akin to amusement flitted across the hazel eyes. Matthew contemplated her for a moment as he took a slow sip of his wine. 'Unlike her daughter, by the looks of things.'

Unabashed, she held his gaze. 'Not all women are incapable of functioning without some man to tell them what to do. Some of us, I'm happy to say, can manage perfectly without a man.'

'Congratulations.' But it was not a compliment, more a taunt.

'No doubt your vanity makes it hard for you to believe that your sex is not indispensable?'

He simply smiled, a maddeningly complacent smile. 'I have a feeling, Miss Garland, that you're passing judgement on a subject you know nothing about. As the saying goes, one can't miss what one has never had.' He held her eyes. 'Am I not right?'

Olivia flushed, but did not look away. 'Nor does one need to venture into the desert to know that it contains nothing but sand.' She smiled, pleased with this wisdom. But he had the last word.

'There may be oil beneath the desert. Riches beyond dreams. And magnificent sunsets over the dunes. It's only the very shortsighted, Miss Garland, who see nothing but sand.'

The philosophical tenor of the conversation abated slightly as they moved on to the second course. The more immediate and palpable attractions of an inch-thick *entrecôte* steak, garnished with mustard sauce, seemed to have largely diverted Matthew's attention as Olivia picked half-heartedly at her suddenly tasteless baby chicken.

However, she was aware, more than once, that the hazel eyes were watching her. And she seemed to catch, now and then, a glimpse of that serious quality of before. Then he would abruptly look away or smile one of those taunting smiles, and she would feel the irritation in her flicker again. There were no hidden depths to Matthew Jordan. He was precisely the vain, self-centred chauvinist that he appeared on the surface to be.

'Would *madame* and *monsieur* care to order a dessert?' The waiter paused as he cleared away their plates.

Olivia began to shake her head. Pointedly she glanced at her watch. 'Just coffee for me, thank you.' She had already had more than enough of this farce. There was no point in prolonging it. But her companion was evidently in no hurry to be on his way. Disregarding her unsubtle hint, he ordered a fresh fruit salad and brandy to follow.

'I see your asceticism extends into all areas of your life,' he observed amusedly as she sat fiddling with her cup of black coffee while he poured a generous helping of fresh cream over a generous helping of fruit salad.

She frowned at him disapprovingly. 'I see it extends into none of yours.'

He gave her a shrewd look. 'I believe the pleasures of life are there to be enjoyed. To the full.'

'No doubt.' An image of the blonde Celine flashed not inappropriately to mind. Olivia smiled thinly at him. 'Please don't let me keep you from them. I'm sure you're had enough business for one night.'

He smiled back, understanding. 'Don't worry, Miss Garland, you're keeping me from nothing that won't wait. Besides, I'm in no hurry. I happen to be quite enjoying myself.'

Yes, thought Olivia sourly, at my expense. What he was enjoying was the fact that she was hating every second of this ordeal. Tight-lipped, she waited while the waiter at length removed the dessert dish, then returned a moment later with fresh coffee for her and a balloon of Rémy Martin which he set in front of Matthew Jordan.

Unhurriedly, Matthew raised the glass between long, tanned fingers, so that the curve of the balloon rested comfortably in the palm of his hand. He swirled the amber liquid round, taking time to warm it before he drank, his eyes fixed on the stiff, upright figure opposite, a light smile hovering around his lips. 'So, Miss Garland,' he said at last, 'what do you think of my latest offer?'

'I find it unacceptable. Just like the others.'

He drank briefly, his eyes unwavering. 'You really want your company back?'

Did he really need to ask? 'I'll settle for nothing less.'

He drank again, allowing the fiery cognac to roll against his palate for a moment before swallowing. Then he leaned back slightly in his seat and regarded her through lowered lids. 'Perhaps, after all, a way can be found.'

Olivia's heart leapt to her throat. Sudden optimism surged inside her. She leaned towards him, her blue eyes bright. Hadn't she known he had something up his sleeve? 'Tell me how?' she demanded now.

He took another slow mouthful of his drink and regarded her over the top of the glass. 'As I already explained to you, my uncle Julius's clause is watertight. Only Jordan family members may hold any part of the company. And the definition of what constitutes family is very carefully defined . . .'

Olivia nodded impatiently. 'I know.' He seemed to be circling, avoiding the point, deliberately delaying the moment of truth.

'It covers brothers, sisters, nephews, cousins . . .'

He paused.

She waited.

'And wives.'

'Wives?' She stared back at him in total incomprehension. 'Wives?' she repeated once again.

Matthew Jordan continued to watch her over the top of his glass. The expression in the deep hazel eyes was oddly flat, unreadable. 'If you were my wife,' he clarified, 'you would qualify under the clause.'

For a moment Olivia could only stare at him, totally, utterly taken aback. A mixture of horror and incredulity went through her at the very thought. 'But I'm not,' she said at last.

'You could be.'

She gave a small, embarrassed laugh, wondering if the wine had gone to her head. Had he actually said what she'd thought—or was her imagination playing tricks? She swallowed drily. 'What's that supposed to mean?'

He laid down his glass, leaned towards her and elaborated slowly and extremely soberly—though it still felt as though the world had gone crazy as she listened to him say, 'My dear Miss Garland, what it means is that I'm prepared to give you your company back. On one condition.' He paused. 'On condition that you agree to marry me.'

CHAPTER THREE

OLIVIA was grateful that they were seated in a discreet corner of the restaurant. At least no one could see the look of total imbecility that had settled on her face. She gaped at Matthew Jordan, wondering if this was some kind of joke. 'Are you out of your mind?' she demanded.

He smiled a composed smile. 'I don't think so,' he said.

'You're seriously proposing that I marry you in order to get Garland's back?'

He nodded. 'There's no other way.' Then he leaned back and added reasonably, 'Regard it simply as a business move. You are a businesswoman, after all, as you keep reminding me. We need only remain married long enough to make the thing look respectable—say, six months or so. I sign over the company to you, then we divorce and you and your brother have got what you want.'

So it was not a forever-after proposal of marriage. At least that made it slightly less bizarre. A business move, he had said. And, as long as he kept his side of the bargain, she could see that there was much to be gained.

As though reading her mind, he went on to inform her, 'I'm sure the terms of the contract could be drawn up privately between our lawyers beforehand to the satisfaction of both of us. Just in case you're worried that I might try to back out of the deal.'

'The thought had occurred to me.' Though there was something more sinister on her mind. A question that, should she ever in her wildest nightmares seriously consider such a deal, would definitely need answering. 'Why?' she put to him now. 'You're as much a businessman as I'm a businesswoman. What would you be getting out of such a deal?'

He smiled one of those irritating, superior smiles. 'Don't you think that being married to such a woman as yourself, even for so brief a period, would be reward enough for any man?'

Olivia looked back at him, poker-faced, unamused by his predictable gibe. 'What I think,' she shot back at him caustically, 'is that a hard-nosed businessman like yourself would never contemplate a contract of any kind—let alone one as dubious as this—unless he had something very substantial to gain from it for himself.'

He shrugged. 'OK, I have my reasons. But I prefer to keep them to myself.'

'Why?' Now she was suspicious. 'Do you have something to hide?'

A look of total inscrutability settled on the strong-boned face. 'I think all that need concern you, Miss Garland, is your own position in this issue—and the benefits that you and your brother will derive.'

He was talking as though she had already agreed. Without hesitation, she put him right. 'Oh, don't worry, Mr Jordan. My interest is purely academic. I wouldn't seriously entertain your proposal for a minute.'

Matthew shrugged again with apparent indifference. 'It's the only way you'll get Garland's back.'

Quite possibly. But there were limits to the lengths to which even she was prepared to go. 'It's a preposterous suggestion,' she insisted. Just the thought of it made her shudder.

'Preposterous or no, it's your only chance.' An amused smile flitted across his face. 'I certainly have no intention of making a similar proposal to your brother.'

Very funny. Trust him to make a joke out of it. As she struggled to think up some crushing rejoinder, he turned to catch the waiter's eye and signalled for the bill. 'If you want Garland's back as badly as you say, you would be wise to think seriously about my offer.'

Then, as the waiter came and laid the bill, enclosed in a discreet folder, in front of him, he reached for his pocket-book and smiled a knowing smile. 'For those things one wants badly in life, there's always a price to be paid. In this case, it's up to you to decide whether or not you're prepared to pay it.'

He slipped a gold American Express card from the wallet and laid it, with a brief glance at the bill, on the folder. 'I'll give you forty-eight hours, Miss Garland. If I don't hear from you by then, I shall assume that my proposal is unacceptable and that will be the end of that.

'Think well,' he counselled, regarding her coolly. 'You won't get a second chance.'

*   *   *

For the next two days Olivia could think of nothing else.

The man must be crazy, she kept telling herself. Who else but a madman would propose such a thing? And, since she was in full possession of her own mental faculties, the only decent and sensible thing to do was just to forget the whole idea.

But that wasn't an easy option either. How could she reject out of hand the only real hope that she had? Matthew Jordan hadn't been lying when he'd told her there was no other way. Her solicitor's investigations into the details of Jordan's charter had revealed that what he had told her about Great-Uncle Julius's devious little clause had been absolutely right. Though Jordan Electronics in its entirety could be taken over by outside interests, individual bits of it could not.

She was totally blocked, it seemed.

The only person Olivia had mentioned Matthew Jordan's proposal to was Lewis. His habitually composed features had creased into an expression of disbelief and consternation that more or less exactly mirrored her own shell-shocked emotions.

'Was he *serious*?' he had demanded with an incredulous frown. 'Why would he want to do such a thing?' Adding hastily, diplomatically, 'I don't wish to be offensive. You are, after all, a highly attractive and eligible young woman.' He carefully smoothed his iron-grey hair. 'But it does all seem just a little bit sudden.'

Olivia had smiled. 'My feelings exactly. I just wish I knew what was behind this move.' Perhaps, if she could figure out his motives, she would be in a better position to decide.

It was almost as though Lewis had read her mind. The wily accountant smiled. 'You've got until tomorrow evening, you say? Relax, Miss Garland. Just leave it to me.'

It was on the afternoon of the following day, just hours before Jordan's deadline expired, and Olivia was down at The Gallery, sorting out a batch of newly arrived paintings. Suddenly the phone rang. Jeffrey, her assistant, answered it.

'It's Mr Ottley for you,' he told her. 'He says something important's come up.'

Anxiously Olivia grabbed the phone. 'Lewis, what's happening?' she wanted to know.

'Miss Garland, I think you should come over straight away. I've just made a rather interesting discovery that explains Matthew Jordan's proposal to you.'

Olivia felt her heart give a lurch. 'I'll be over in ten minutes,' she promised. Then, as she hung up, she turned to Jeffrey with an apologetic frown. 'Lewis wants to see me urgently. Can you cope with this on your own?'

Jeffrey nodded and grinned. 'Of course,' he assured her unnecessarily. For she knew full well that the energetic Jeffrey could have run The Gallery single-handed.

'I'll be back as soon as I can,' she promised, already grabbing her coat. Then she was dashing headlong out of the door, heading for her car.

Lewis was waiting for her in the entrance hall, an unaccustomed gleam of excitement in his eyes. 'Come.' He propelled her urgently through the swing doors and along the corridor to his office. 'You'll never guess what our solicitors have turned up,' he told her once they were safely inside.

Olivia poised herself on the edge of one of the chairs as Lewis sat down opposite her. 'What?' she demanded—and waited, her stomach churning with anticipation.

As Lewis leaned towards her and began to speak, he twisted the middle-finger ring on his right hand —always a sign of tension. 'When our solicitors were investigating the Jordan charter to check up on that exclusion clause, quite by accident they turned up something else.' His face beamed with conspiracy. 'Another unexpected little clause in the charter that explains everything quite beautifully.'

Olivia was almost jumping out of her skin with curiosity. 'Get to the point, Lewis,' she told him.

He took a deep breath. 'It's all so simple.' Again that gleam shone in his eyes. 'The reason that Matthew Jordan proposed to you is quite simply that he needs a wife.'

Olivia blinked. 'Needs a wife? What on earth do you mean by that?'

'I mean, Miss Garland, that his notorious great-uncle Julius had inserted in the charter another little clause that his duplicitous great-nephew conveniently omitted to tell you about . . .' He smiled smugly as he played his trump card. 'It transpires that control of the company can only be assumed by a married man. Uncle Julius, it appears, was a man of the strictest Victorian principles, a firm believer in the family man. Matthew Jordan is entitled to be company chief *only* if he has a wife.'

Olivia frowned across at him, barely comprehending. 'But that can't be true,' she protested. For once Lewis had got his facts wrong. 'He's already taken over the company and he hasn't got a wife.'

'Ah . . .' Lewis held up his hand and confidently shook his greying head. 'The clause gives him six months to rectify the situation. If, by the time that period elapses, he's still unmarried, control of the company passes to the next in line.'

'And who would that be?'

'According to my information, a younger cousin who at the moment plays a somewhat peripheral role in the running of Jordan Electronics. He's already married with a couple of children.'

For a long moment Olivia stared at him, unable to take in this astounding news. 'You mean he really would lose control of Jordan's if he didn't get married within six months?'

'Less than *three* months now,' Lewis corrected her. 'Remember, he inherited from his uncle Roland back in January.'

Suddenly, as Lewis had warned her, it was all falling neatly into place. Matthew Jordan had as much to gain from this marriage of convenience as she did herself. It was hard, not to say impossible, to imagine him voluntarily relinquishing control of Jordan's. Or of anything else, come to that. If she were to accept his preposterous proposal, they would be entering the deal on equal ground.

Maybe, she found herself wondering wildly, the arrangement might be feasible, after all.

Lewis was watching her with bright, expectant eyes. 'This gives you the leverage you need, Miss

Garland. You're in a position to dictate your terms.'

That was undoubtedly true, but Olivia was still unsure. She smiled weakly at him. 'But marriage, Lewis . . . to a man like that! It's such a terrifyingly drastic step.'

He leaned towards her sympathetically. 'Miss Garland, you know I've been behind you all the way in your fight to get Garland's back.' He paused as she nodded, acknowledging the absolute truth of his claim. No mere employee could have been expected to support her so loyally. The merger, after all, had brought no personal disadvantage to Lewis. And, in spite of the immediate discomfort of the appointment of McKay, a man of Lewis Ottley's talents could only ultimately benefit from being a part of so huge an organisation.

'I know that, and I appreciate it,' she told him.

He frowned and fiddled uneasily with the middle-finger signet ring. 'If there was any other possibility left open to us now, I would counsel you to hang on and try.' He shrugged a shrug of bleak despair. 'But we're up against a brick wall now. This really is the only chance we've got.'

Olivia sighed and glanced away, recognising the cruel truth of his words.

'It would be a sacrifice on your part, I know. But remember, it would only be a temporary arrangement.' He paused. 'Think of your brother. You know as well as I do that it would break his heart to lose Garland's for good.'

'I know, I know.' In anguish, Olivia dropped

her head into her hands.

Lewis sighed sympathetically. 'But the decision has to be yours, Miss Garland. And whatever you decide, I'll be on your side.'

'Thank you.' She raised her head and took a deep breath and stole a tentative glance at her watch. There were still a couple of hours to go before Matthew Jordan's deadline expired. With a sigh, she started to stand up. 'If you don't mind, I'd like to go now and have a quiet think by myself.'

'Of course.' Respectfully, Lewis rose to his feet.

'I'll make my own way out.' At the door, Olivia paused. 'And I'll let you know what I decide.'

Difficult decisions should always be made in surroundings that inspired peace of mind. Almost automatically now, Olivia found herself driving north till she came to a favourite old family picnic spot, overlooking the River Dee.

It was deserted now as she parked the car, the sun already beginning to set, fiery-red, in a clear April sky. She leaned against the steering-wheel, stared outside and tried to straighten the jumble in her head.

The trouble was that, as so often, her head was in open conflict with her heart. Her head said: be cool. Treat it as a business move. But her heart was telling her: beware! Yet her ultimate consideration had to be Richard. Would he ever forgive her if she were to pass up this final chance to save Garland's—and, with it, his future?

The weight of responsibility was crushing, but the fear she felt still held her back. For, as she had confided to Lewis, it would be a terrifying step to take. To be thrust into a state of marriage—a state she had never really seriously considered before—with, of all men in the world, one she detested so profoundly.

A chill went through her. She closed her eyes. Was she really tough enough to make that ultimate sacrifice?

An hour later she drove back to her flat and poured herself a very stiff drink. Then she took from her bag the business card that Matthew Jordan had given her and dialled the number with trembling fingers. With any luck, she was praying, he would already have gone home and she could leave her message on his answering machine.

But, almost instantly, his cool tones answered. 'Matthew Jordan here.'

Olivia hesitated. Then, 'It's me, Olivia Garland,' she said nervously.

'Miss Garland, what a nice surprise!' His tone changed slightly. 'What can I do for you?'

For one precarious moment Olivia's nerve almost deserted her. She took a quick swig of her drink and resisted the temptation to hang up. Instead, in a voice that she could barely recognise, that seemed to belong to someone else, she told him, 'About that proposal of yours. I've decided to accept.'

'I want one thing to be absolutely clear. The only reason I've agreed to enter into this ridiculous contract is that I know about the secret marriage clause. I do you a favour, you do me a favour.

Strictly business,' Olivia spelled out.

They were sitting in the immense drawing-room of Matthew Jordan's Hertfordshire home, just a few miles outside St Albans. Olivia had flown down that afternoon, in one of Jordan Electronics' company jets, to spend the weekend—at Matthew's behest. 'So that,' as he had put it, 'we can finalise the deal.'

He was looking casual in grey trousers and an open-necked blue check shirt as he lounged in one of the huge velvet armchairs that were scattered about the elegant room; she considerably less at ease as she perched on the edge of her own chair opposite, her slim legs crossed decorously at the ankle, her charcoal skirt adjusted over her knees.

A woman who was evidently his housekeeper had brought them tea and biscuits on a tray, but Olivia was feeling far too nervous even to have sampled hers as yet. Matthew, contrarily, was helping himself to a second cup. He said with a faint smile, 'That was very clever of your Mr Ottley to find out about old Uncle Julius's secret marriage clause.'

'Of course he's clever. That's why the company employs him.' She threw him a derisive look. 'Why didn't you just tell me in the first place what your proposal was all about, instead of trying to pretend you were doing me some sort of big-hearted favour?'

He leaned unselfconsciously back in his chair and regarded her through amused hazel eyes. 'Just my devious nature, I guess. I like to play my cards close to my chest.'

'You also like to have the upper hand,' Olivia
enlightened him coolly. She could see through
him as clearly as a pane of glass. 'You like to feel
that you're in control. Well, you can forget any
such notions now.' She deliberately straightened
her shoulders. 'We go into this deal as equals.'

'My feelings entirely.' He smiled enigmatically
and ran his fingers through his thick, dark hair.
'I've always believed that marriage is a contract
into which two people should enter strictly on
equal terms.'

Olivia grimaced at the mention of the word
'marriage'. 'I prefer to refer to our contract as a
business arrangement. After all, that's all it is.'

'Absolutely,' he agreed.

She held his eyes, not quite daring to come
straight out with what it was she wanted to say.
And she was suddenly acutely, burningly aware of
the vibrantly male presence of him—the glimpse of
muscular, dark-tanned chest revealed at the open
neck of his shirt, the broad shoulders, strong
forearms and the long, hard-thighed legs that were
stretched out casually in front of him.

She touched the high-buttoned neck of her
blouse and repeated, 'A *business* arrangement. I
want to be quite unambiguous that that's all it is.'

'What else?' He drank and laid aside his empty
cup before adding with amused sarcasm, 'One
could scarcely describe it as a love-match, after all.'

'And I have your word that, as soon as
Garland's has been transferred, divorce proceedings will begin?'

'You have my word. Though only after a

respectable period of time. I think we've already agreed on six months.'

Olivia paled at the thought. It sounded like an eternity. But she nodded, then added suspiciously, 'You're sure there's not some other secret clause that requires you to remain married?' It would be absolutely unbearable if he were to renege on their deal.

But he shook his head. 'I'm afraid that was one eventuality that Great-Uncle Julius failed to foresee. In his day, divorce was less common than it is now. People tended to marry for life. My uncle made the profound error of assuming such attitudes would endure.'

Olivia felt a sharp stab of discomfort at his words. She had been brought up to believe the same. And she did. Marriage should be for life. Which was yet another reason why she continued to feel uneasy about what she was about to do. Unfortunately, she consoled herself, it was some-times necessary to sacrifice one's ideals for the sake of a greater good. And this marriage would be no marriage at all. Only on paper would it qualify as such.

She told him, 'I'd like a written guarantee that no such secret clause exists.'

'You shall have it. Though, naturally, you will understand that no official agreement can be made in advance regarding our intention to divorce. That would invalidate the marriage.'

She nodded. 'Yes. Unfortunately.'

'You'll just have to trust me, I'm afraid.'

Not something that came naturally.

'And, likewise, I'll just have to trust you. For all I know, when the time comes you might decide to change your mind.' Matthew smiled strangely. 'You might decide that, after all, you rather like being married to me.'

Olivia almost laughed out loud. The man's self-delusion knew no bounds! 'Don't worry,' she scoffed. 'That's one thing you definitely needn't fear. As soon as the six months are up, you won't see my heels for dust!'

'Good.' The dark head nodded his approval. 'That's precisely what I'm banking on.'

Feeling herself relax just a bit, Olivia sat back in her chair and reached for her untouched cup of tea. She drank, regarding Matthew Jordan over the rim. 'There's still one thing that puzzles me. Why did you choose me? I'm sure a man like yourself would have no great difficulty in finding a wife.' Someone, she added to herself, who would provide him with a somewhat more satisfying six months than she intended to do. An image of the docile, attentive Celine flashed immediately to mind. 'Your secretary, for example. I'm sure she would have been happy to oblige.'

Without a trace of modesty, he assured her, 'Yes, I'm sure she would.' Then he smiled. 'But, unlike you, she wouldn't have been so easy to get rid of when the time came.' The long-lashed hazel eyes held hers. 'That's why you're perfect for such a purpose. Like me, you see this as a straight-forward business deal.' He straightened and leaned towards her, causing her involuntarily to draw back her knees. 'And now I suggest we tackle the details. Dates, that sort of thing. The marriage should take place as quickly as possible.' He threw her a calculating look. 'The sooner it's started, the sooner it's over. And that's what we both want, isn't it?'

Olivia nodded woodenly, trying to hide the trepidation she felt.

'I'm sure we could manage to have everything arranged for the week after next.'

So soon? She felt a cold sensation shiver inside.

'Naturally, since you'll be staying here, you'll have to make arrangements for your art gallery. What about your assistant? Will he be able to run it while you're gone?'

Olivia nodded. 'That's no problem.'

'Good. And naturally we shall keep the details of our little arrangement to ourselves.' As she flushed slightly and glanced away, he added suspiciously, 'Or have you already made them public knowledge?'

'I've told Lewis,' she admitted.

'Ottley?'

She nodded. 'But don't worry, I can trust him. He won't spread it around.'

He seemed to consider this for a moment. 'Make sure he doesn't. Not for the sake of our marriage, more for the sake of our divorce. I'm sure neither of us would want anything to get in the way of that.'

Nothing surer.

He stood up. 'And now I'll show you round the house.' As she hesitated he added, 'After all, it's going to be your home too—at least, for the next six months.'

Reluctantly Olivia got to her feet, smoothing the skirt of her charcoal suit—and all at once was uncomfortably aware of his gaze difting downwards to her breasts. Then she recoiled in sudden horror as he reached out one hand to touch her blouse. As she jerked away—'What the devil do you think you're doing?'—his free hand came out to grab her by the arm, preventing her from moving away.

'Nothing to worry about.' He smiled. 'Just one of the buttons of your blouse undone.' And with deft, unhurried fingers he proceeded to complete his interrupted task. 'That's better.' He held her eyes as, lightly, the side of his hand brushed against her breast. 'We can't have you exposing yourself. Someone might realise you're a woman.'

Olivia's face was flaming as he continued to hold her there, the fingers clamped around her arm like imprisoning bands of steel. And there was something almost suffocating about his nearness as he looked down at her with a slow, mocking smile. 'My dear Olivia,' he told her, addressing her informally for the very first time, 'you really mustn't let such a small intimacy upset you. After all,' he reminded her with relish, 'you and I are practically husband and wife.'

His face was so close to hers that she could see quite clearly the dark amber flecks in the deep hazel irises, and she felt her stomach contract in sudden panic as the wide mouth parted in a smile. 'Let me go!' she commanded, struggling futilely as he held her firm, trying to decide just how hard she would hit him if he dared to try to kiss her now.

But she was safe—for the moment, at least. With a shake of his head, Matthew stepped away and abruptly let go his hold on her arm. 'Come, Olivia, let me show you the house.' Then he was leading her across the room, she following at a safe distance behind, her body still trembling with outrage and anger, her heart still clamouring inside.

'Damn you, Matthew Jordan!' she was muttering to herself. 'Don't you dare try another trick like that!'

But all the outrage she could muster somehow couldn't quite dispel the sudden sharp sense of foreboding that she felt.

CHAPTER FOUR

TEN days later, in a register office ceremony in north London, a somewhat tight-lipped and nervous Olivia officially became Mrs Matthew Jordan.

As Matthew had predicted, the whole thing had been organised with alarming speed—a blessing in disguise, Olivia had stoically convinced herself. That way, she hadn't had time to dwell upon the ghastliness of her situation. And, as Matthew had pointed out, the sooner the ordeal was started, the sooner it would be over.

'I'm certain you won't regret it,' Lewis had reassured her kindly when, ashen-faced, she had broken the news to him. 'The six months will be over in no time at all—and look what you'll have gained at the end of it.' With a proud smile he had held out his hand. 'Congratulations, Miss Garland. It's a noble and worthy thing that you're doing.'

Worthy of the Victoria Cross, Olivia was thinking wryly to herself as he added, 'Young Mr Richard will have reason to be grateful to you for the rest of his life.'

But Richard must never know. Not only would it be grossly demeaning to her were her brother to discover the reason behind her sudden marriage, it would also place an unfair debt of gratitude on his young shoulders. As her face changed, Lewis smiled and held up his hands. 'Don't worry, I won't breathe a word. I was talking theoretically.'

'I have your word on that?'

The grey head nodded. 'You know you can trust me.'

All the same, it was with some trepidation that she had phoned Richard at his boarding-school to give him the news. After their mother's regrettable experience with Roland, the Jordans rated no more highly in her brother's book than in her own.

'Good lord,' had been his flat-voiced comment. 'What's with these Jordan men? Haven't they already done enough damage to our family through one marriage? Sorry, Sis, I thought you had better taste.'

Olivia had gritted her teeth, not blaming him one little bit—and secretly very thankful that the wedding would coincide with a school trip to Belgium that Richard had planned. A fact for which he was evidently grateful too. A meeting with his brother-in-law-to-be was quite clearly not at the top of his list.

'I'll try,' had been his unenthusiastic response when Olivia had felt obliged to urge him to visit them some time. And as she laid down the phone she had consoled herself with the thought that at least it would be that much easier when it came to breaking the news of the divorce to him.

But the divorce was still a distressingly long way away. First there was the marriage—and the wedding—to get through.

'Smile, please!'

All around her flashbulbs were popping, and Olivia had a tight smile pinned to her face. As Matthew slipped an arm round her waist, drawing her close in a mock-romantic embrace, she fought the urge to pull away from him and mustered every latent thespian bone in her body to simulate a passable representation of the happy, blushing bride. Then some joker shouted out, 'Kiss the bride!' Inwardly she steeled herself as, with blatant relish, Matthew hastened to oblige.

'Relax!' he admonished her under his breath. 'I'm not going to assault you. Not in front of all these people.'

Olivia smiled a wobbly smile. The truth was that she really had nothing to complain about—at least as far as Matthew's conduct was concerned. Right from the start of this nerve-racking day, he had treated her with perfect chivalry and consideration.

'Darling, you look beautiful,' he had told her before the ceremony, admiring with his eyes the ivory silk suit she had grudgingly splashed out on for the occasion. And though she had known that the gallant remark, along with the accompanying affectionate peck, had been for the benefit of the guests assembled in the flower-festooned register office, she had found his relaxed and easy composure immensely reassuring somehow. The whole wretched business was a ridiculous travesty, but at least he was enabling them to get through it with an outward patina of dignity.

The ceremony itself had been awesomely real.

In the course of the previous, almost entirely

sleepless night, Olivia had convinced herself that the only way to get through it would be by simply switching off. Somehow she would just have to let the whole thing wash over her.

In the event, that had proved impossible to do. Though her surroundings had registered as no more than a blur—as had the faces of the couple of dozen or so guests, most of them friends of Matthew's—the simple but undeniably significant little ceremony and the promises she and Matthew had repeated in turn were awesomely, heartrendingly vivid, etched in sharp relief on her brain.

Real too—too real for comfort—had been the powerful physical presence of the tall, dark-suited man at her side. As he had reached out to take her hand—his touch firm, soft and warm—to slide the narrow gold band on to her finger, she had felt the breath catch in her throat and her heart had seemed to stand still in her breast. At the cool, metallic feel of that golden hoop against her skin, it was as though the enormity of what she was doing had suddenly come home to her.

'Forgive me,' she had whispered soundlessly to some invisible confessor. Then she had closed her eyes, her heartbeat quickening, as Matthew bent to seal the false vows with an equally false kiss.

Afterwards they had driven to his London flat overlooking Regent's Park for a champagne and caviare reception, then stood together, side by side, while flashbulbs popped and guests lined up to offer their felicitations. Felicitations whose evident sincerity had made Olivia squirm inside—

though one set, she had detected without too much difficulty, had most definitely not come from the heart.

'I'd like to wish you both all the best.' From the crowd, a blonde-haired figure in striking scarlet had stepped forward and turned on Olivia a pair of lavishly made-up, wide grey eyes whose cold expression belied the warmth of her words. One person who, quite clearly, was far from enamoured by this hasty union was Matthew's secretary, the geisha-like Celine.

Her fingers were cool, barely making contact with Olivia's as they shook hands. Then, with an ambiguous expression, she turned to Matthew and reached up to kiss him on the cheek. 'Congratulations, Mr Jordan,' she purred. She paused to shoot Olivia a sideways glance. 'I hope you don't mind if I kiss the groom?'

'Not at all.' Do anything you like with him, Olivia added mentally to herself, almost wishing it would not have been improper to make the suggestion out loud. No doubt Matthew would do that for her, she reassured herself, secretly glad to see that he had evidently not broken all bonds with the girl. The more time he spent in the company of the delectable Celine, the less time he would have to bother her.

But it was to Olivia that he was turning now as he stole a quick glance at his watch. 'It's time we thought about leaving. We have a plane to catch.'

Olivia frowned, recalling the way he had sprung his secret plans on her earlier this morning, on her arrival from Chester. 'I hope you've brought your passport with you. I've booked us a week in Paris.'

'Paris?' She'd gaped at him.

'Where better for a honeymoon than the most romantic city in the world?'

'A honeymoon?' The very notion was ridiculous—and, what was more, faintly appalling. 'What do we want a honeymoon for?' she had protested. 'This isn't even going to be a proper marriage!'

Dark hazel eyes had glinted at her from behind thick black lashes. 'You and I know that, my dear Olivia, but the rest of the world is under the impression that this marriage of ours is perfectly regular. For reasons I've already explained, I think it's best that they go on thinking that way. Besides . . .' he threw her a smile, 'is the prospect of a week in Paris really so unappealing?'

Olivia could never have thought she would ever say it, but, quite truthfully, she answered, 'Yes.' Though it was not the prospect of Paris itself, rather the company, that lacked appeal.

And now it was time they were on their way. They were booked on the five o'clock flight and it was already after three. To a boisterous send-off of confetti and rice, they made their way down into the street where Matthew's midnight-blue chauffeured Rolls was waiting.

'Come, Olivia, your carriage awaits.' Playing one final scene to the gallery of photographers, he swept her up into his arms and deposited her bodily inside. And, as he climbed in behind her, Olivia couldn't help quietly congratulating him to

herself. He performed his phoney role of loving
newly-wed so well. Such a consummate and
convincing actor. A fake right down to his
fingertips!

To her relief, however, he dropped the act as
soon as they were away from their guests. On
the journey to Heathrow Airport and for most of
the flight itself he seemed to be in a quiet,
reflective frame of mind. No doubt, in his heart
of hearts, he was looking forward to the months
ahead with no more relish than she was herself.

As the stewardess brought them a mid-air
snack—served on fine white, first-class
porcelain, so different from the economy-class
plastic to which Olivia was accustomed—she
stole a glance at him from the corner of her eye.
He was, after all, just as much a victim of
circumstance as she.

He caught her looking. 'Is everything OK?'

As OK as could be expected in the circumstances. Olivia nodded and answered formally,
'Yes, thank you, quite OK.'

Matthew smiled. 'One down and only a
hundred and seventy-nine to go.'

Olivia frowned, uncomprehending. 'One
what?' she enquired testily, suspecting in the
obtuse remark some secret joke at her expense.
'A hundred and seventy-nine what to go?'

Deliberately he held her eyes. 'Days,' he told
her. 'Of wedded bliss.'

She grimaced across at him, feeling a sudden
sharp plummet of alarm. 'You mean our
business contract,' she corrected him, her voice

and her expression pure, untempered steel.

'My dear Olivia, you're so unromantic!' He threw her one of his mocking smiles. 'I can see that our little Parisian sojourn is going to be completely wasted on you.'

Olivia stared back levelly at him. 'Totally,' she agreed. 'If this so-called honeymoon was really necessary, you could have saved yourself some money and settled for Bognor Regis, as far as I'm concerned.'

Though that wasn't strictly true, she privately conceded as they disembarked at the French capital's elegant Charles de Gaulle Airport and made their way by taxi to the very heart of the ancient city. It was years since Olivia had last visited Paris. She had been barely eighteen when she and Richard had come here on holiday with their parents, and she remembered it as a grandly stylish and rather magical place.

In spite of herself, she pressed against the taxi window now, her excitement growing as they made their way through the hectic evening traffic, round the floodlit Arc de Triomphe, then down the wide, tree-lined Champs Elysées, thronged with boulevard cafés and expensive shops and chic promenading Parisians.

Next thing, she heard Matthew murmur, 'We're here,' as they turned into the forecourt of the city's most famous and exclusive hotel.

'Nothing but the best, I see,' she said cuttingly to cover her awe.

He merely smiled that infuriating smile as he leaned across her to open up the door. 'But of course,' he answered. 'Nothing but the best for my bride.'

Olivia avoided looking at him as she climbed out, reluctant to let him see just how much his banter got to her. For she knew he was only doing it to annoy her. This 'my bride' routine was just his way of amusing himself at her expense.

As a man in hotel uniform came hurrying down the steps to gather up their bags, she took a deep breath and composed herself. She must try not to let him upset her and never allow him to gain the upper hand. Otherwise the next six months could prove to be a living hell.

Once more gallant, Matthew took her arm and led her into the enormous foyer—all plush velvet sofas, crystal chandeliers and gigantic gilded mirrors. 'Have you ever stayed here before?' he enquired casually, noting how she looked around.

With a wry smile, Olivia shook her head. 'I had afternoon coffee here once.' On that holiday with her parents, she remembered Richard, her mother and herself—even on holiday her father had spent little time with them!—passing an agreeable couple of hours spinning out a pot of coffee and a couple of slices of gâteau that had cost more than a three-course meal in Chester, while, as her mother had put it, they had watched 'how the other half lives'. At the time it had never crossed Olivia's mind that one day, even very temporarily, she might belong to that privileged 'other half'.

Inwardly, she sighed. What a pity that her sudden elevation in life had been made under duress, and at the hands of a man she so devoutly disliked.

Feeling the knot in her stomach tighten, she stood to one side, but within hearing distance, as Matthew crossed to the reception desk. This was the moment of truth she had been dreading, when the details of a somewhat crucial subject that she hadn't so far dared to raise would finally be revealed to her. Namely, their sleeping arrangements for the next seven nights. In spite of this embarrassing masquerade as newly-weds, surely he had had the good taste to book them into separate rooms?

To her sudden acute distress, it appeared that he had not. An apprehensive chill crept through her bones as she heard the desk clerk politely acknowledge him. 'Ah, *bienvenu*, Monsieur Jordan!' Then, with a discreet smile and a glance in her own direction, he added in English, 'The *garçon* will show you to the bridal suite.'

Olivia's heart dropped to her shoes. The bridal suite, indeed! Hadn't Matthew taken the joke far enough?

Deliberately, she kept her eyes from his face as he took her arm and steered her across the huge marble hall to where the uniformed boy was waiting by the lifts. And all the way up she stared at the floor, carefully keeping her anger in check. Inside, she was boiling. How dared he subject her to this charade?

At last, at the end of a plushly carpeted

corridor, they reached the gilded door of the
bridal suite. *'Madame . . . monsieur . . .'* The boy
pushed the door open and stood aside.

The room beyond was sumptuous, like
something out of a fairy-tale—vast, furnished
with exquisite taste in shades of rose and powder-
blue. The delicate furniture, Olivia guessed, was
probably genuine Louis Quinze, the curtains and
draperies sheeny silk, the rugs on the floor
priceless Chinese.

But what totally dominated the entire room and
instantly drew her uneasy eye was a draped and
swathed four-poster bed that seemed to shimmer
beneath the starry chandelier.

A more romantic setting for a honeymoon was
scarcely imaginable. What a waste, thought
Olivia to herself, that none of it was destined to
be put to the use that its designers had intended.

The uniformed boy was showing them round,
pushing open the door of the equally opulent
adjoining bathroom with its solid gold fittings,
sunken bath and separate jacuzzi.

'Et le salon.' Now he was opening another door
and leading them into the room beyond—a large
sitting-room, comfortably furnished with a sofa
and armchairs and a mahogany writing-desk in
one corner.

At this revelation, Olivia felt some of her
tension slacken. So there were two quite separate
rooms, after all. It looked as though she had
misjudged him. He had evidently taken a suite
for the sake of appearances, knowing that, in fact,
it would suit their purposes very well. The silk

brocade-upholstered sofa looked positively spartan when compared with the bed in the room next door, but no doubt it would be adequately comfortable. She allowed herself a sigh of relief. He had almost certainly slept on worse in his time.

With a bow and a fifty-franc tip, the boy was taking his leave of them. *'Merci, monsieur. Madame. Bonsoir.'* With a final bow, he closed the door.

'Alone at last!' With one of those amused, faintly mocking smiles that Olivia was growing to know so well, Matthew turned to look at her. 'Shall we unpack and order something from room service, or would you prefer to go out for a meal?'

Automatically, Olivia glanced at her watch, aware that she was both hungry and tired. It was just after nine. After all the excitement and upheaval of the day, not to mention her previous sleepless night, she didn't much feel like going out. 'I'd be quite happy to eat here,' she replied, stifling a yawn. Then go straight to bed, she added to herself, preferring not to express the sentiment aloud lest it come out sounding ambiguous. Let there be no ambiguity whatsoever on that particular point.

'Precisely my feelings.' Matthew was peeling off his jacket and tossing it on to a chair. He crossed to where the porter had laid their cases, unzipped his and quickly began unpacking his things and hanging them in the wardrobe. Aware of her eyes watching him, he glanced round at her over his shoulder. 'This is your job,' he told her with an ambiguous smile, 'but, just this once, I'll let you off.'

'My job?'

'It's a wife's job to unpack for her husband. Don't you know about things like that?'

'No, I don't, as a matter of fact.' Though the truth was, she had learned—and rejected—such habits from childhood, from her mother. And she had no intention of back-tracking now. Matthew Jordan might be used to grovelling women, but she would never play the geisha for him. 'There's one thing we should get straight right from the very start,' she told him in a clipped and hostile voice. 'I will not be performing any wifely duties for you at any time over the next six months.'

Her rebuke was water off a duck's back. He finished unpacking and tossed her a smile. 'However, to make up for the disappointment of not unpacking for me, I'll leave you to order dinner for us. I'm off to have a shower.' He paused and handed her the room-service menu that stood propped on the dressing-table to one side. 'I'll have the steak *au poivre.* That's always excellent here. And some of their goose liver pâté to start. And order a bottle of their best Pommard—if that's to your taste.'

He threw her a deliberately aggravating wink as he headed towards the bathroom door. 'You choose anything you like. Do you think you can manage that?'

Olivia almost threw the menu after him as the bathroom door closed behind him with a click. Of all the arrogant, overbearing, insufferable individuals! Exasperation rendered her almost speechless as, very slowly, she counted up to ten.

Still, look on the bright side, she consoled herself. Think how much more dreadful things would be if you were really, seriously married to him. For life. She shuddered at the thought. Pity the poor woman who ever ended up having to contemplate such a fate!

She flicked through the impressive room-service menu and decided to go along with Matthew's choice. A nice big juicy steak was precisely what she felt like right now. Since she couldn't sink her teeth into him, it would make a passable substitute!

She had just laid down the phone and was setting about unpacking her own few things when the bathroom door opened and Matthew emerged, clad only in the hotel's monogrammed white towelling robe, the clothes he had been wearing earlier draped casually over one arm. With the sureness of one who is used to spending a great deal of time in top-class hotels, he crossed to a drawer and pulled out a plastic laundry bag into which he deposited shirt, underwear and socks.

Olivia kept her eyes averted as he then moved to the wardrobe to hang up his suit. 'As you'll have noticed,' he commented over his shoulder, 'I've used only a small part of the hanging space. Feel free to use the rest.'

'So kind!' Her tone was sarcastic as she waited for him to remove himself before carrying over her couple of skirts and blouses and arranging them on hangers. Too bad there weren't separate wardrobes, she was thinking moodily as she pushed them to the end of the rail, as far away from his things as she could possibly get. There was something all too intimate about their clothes hanging together, side by side, in the same wardrobe. Which was why she had left her underwear and her night things discreetly in her bag. Matthew had brought no night things, she had observed. Thank heavens he would be locked away safely in the other room for the night!

He had deposited himself in the meantime on one of the delicate bedroom chairs, his broad, muscular frame providing an uneasy contrast with its apparent frailty, and he was leafing through one of the entertainment guides that were strewn about the room. 'We must go to the Lido while we're here,' he told her, glancing up. 'It's usually booked up for weeks ahead, but I'm sure the hotel can fix us up.'

Olivia regarded him with cool disapproval. 'Get them to book you a table if you wish, but count me out. An evening ogling half-naked women doesn't count as entertainment in my book.'

He smiled, amused. 'Dear, dear! Quite the little puritan. But never mind. You can concentrate your attentions on the food, I'll do all the ogling.'

No doubt he would. Olivia remained standing in the middle of the room, not quite certain where to put herself, acutely conscious of the semi-clad figure eyeing her with amusement from the gilt armchair. The deep V of the loosely tied robe revealed a disconcertingly eye-catching expanse of smoothly muscled, dark-tanned chest, while the hem that stopped short above his knees exposed to perfection a pair of shapely, hair-roughened male legs.

Olivia hadn't even removed the jacket of her suit. She thrust her hands into its pockets now and looked down at him censoriously. 'Don't you think you ought to get dressed? They'll be here with our dinner soon.'

Matthew raised one dark eyebrow at her and stretched his legs more comfortably. 'I am dressed, my dear Olivia—perfectly adequately. Don't worry, those room-service boys have seen a lot more shocking things in their time than yours truly in his dressing-gown.' The deep hazel eyes roamed over her attire. 'Why don't you follow my example and slip into something more comfortable?' He nodded in the direction of the bathroom. 'There's another robe in there.'

He had to be joking! Olivia had no more intention of parading around semi-clothed in front of him that she had of dangling from the chandelier.

Pointedly, she sat down on the edge of one of the high-backed chairs that lined the wall and crossed her legs primly at the ankle. 'I'm already quite comfortable enough,' she told him, though it wasn't really true. The centrally heated room was extremely warm, and she could feel the silk blouse beneath her jacket sticking to her back. But she was damned if she would shed a single stitch until he was safely asleep in the other room.

Dinner arrived promptly and was served in the *salon*. And it was absolutely delicious—the *pâté* exquisite, the steak melt-in-the-mouth and the wine full-bodied and mellow.

Away from the bedroom, Olivia started to relax a bit. Between the *pâté* and the steak, she had finally succumbed to the central heating and removed the jacket of her suit. Without any immediately dire results. Matthew had simply smiled. 'Hot, huh? I told you, you should have changed.'

Throughout the entire meal, in fact, he was remarkably civil, keeping the conversation to a comfortably non-personal exchange of stories about Paris and hotels abroad. And as he put to her his plans for the week ahead—a trip up the Eiffel Tower, a visit to the Louvre—Olivia began to feel the tiniest spark of enthusiasm come alive. And why not? she rationalised to herself. It was a long time since she'd had a holiday, and Paris was one of the world's most exciting cities. Why shouldn't she enjoy it?

'I don't suppose I can tempt you to indulge in a dessert?' he enquired as they pushed aside their empty steak plates.

Olivia shook her head. 'No, thanks.' She had already eaten more than enough, and she could feel tiredness creeping over her.

'Coffee?'

Again she shook her head. 'I think I'll skip that as well. I'd just like to have a shower now and turn in, if you don't mind.'

'I don't mind at all.' He stretched briefly and yawned. 'I'm pretty tired, too. It's been quite a day.' He ran long, tanned fingers over his hair. 'I think you're right—it's time for bed.'

Awkwardly, Olivia started to stand up. 'OK, I'll leave you, then.' She gathered up her jacket from the back of the chair and avoided looking at him as she asked, 'Do you want to use the bathroom first?'

Matthew shook his head. 'No need,' he said.

'Very well.' She turned and headed for the bedroom door. 'In that case, I'll say goodnight.'

Once on the other side of the door, she let out a huge sigh of relief. So he was capable of acting like a gentleman, after all. She kicked off her shoes and crossed to the bathroom. Instead of the shower she'd mentioned, she'd treat herself to a relaxing ten minutes in the jacuzzi. That would give Matthew ample time to help himself to a couple of blankets from the wardrobe and make himself comfortable on the sofa next door. She smiled to herself. He had said he was tired too. By the time she emerged from her bath he would probably be sound asleep.

The jacuzzi was delicious. Olivia leaned back and closed her eyes, loving the sensuous, relaxing play of the warm jets against her naked body. One down and how many more left to go, had he said? Too many—but be grateful for small mercies, she reminded herself. Every day ticked off the grand total was a day to celebrate.

Out of the bath, she rubbed herself dry and tied a soft pink towel around her bosom, then carefully unpinned her glossy dark hair and shook it loose about her shoulders. As she glanced at her reflection in the mirror—at the ivory-skinned shoulders and throat and the long, shapely, slender legs peeping out from beneath the towel that barely skimmed the tops of her thighs—she had to stifle a sleepy yawn. Suddenly the thought of that huge silk bed, just waiting for her on the other side of the door, was enormously appealing. She couldn't wait to get into it. She felt as though she could sleep for a week.

As soon as she opened the bathroom door, however, she realised that something was amiss. All the lights in the bedroom beyond had mysteriously been dimmed. Olivia frowned. What was going on? Then, cautiously, she stepped into the room.

The next instant she stopped in her tracks, all her tiredness instantly fleeing from her. In its place, mingled horror and outrage were suddenly burning through her veins. For lying casually on the bed, his dark head propped against the snow-white pillows, was Matthew, and he was smiling strangely.

'At last!' The dark eyes caressed her semi-naked form as with one hand he flicked back the bedclothes and invited, 'Come, my bride. Come and join me.'

CHAPTER FIVE

OLIVIA felt her jaw drop open. Her feet seemed riveted to the floor. 'What the . . .?' she started to protest, her cheeks burning as bright pink as the towel wrapped scantily around her naked form.

Then, as Matthew continued to watch her from the bed, still smiling that strangely alarming smile as he leaned forward and held out his hand towards her—'Come, 'Olivia. Come and join me . . .'—all at once she was spinning on her heel and hurtling back through the bathroom door.

With trembling fingers she tore from its hook the thick white towelling robe that was hanging on the back of the door, then struggled hastily into it and pulled the belt tight at the waist. Whatever bizarre intention had suddenly entered Matthew's head, she would feel better equipped to deal with it if she was properly dressed.

As she strode back into the bedroom, shoulders squared, chin held high, ready for a confrontation, he had already risen from the bed and was standing, hands in the pockets of his own towelling robe, half-way to the bathroom door. He turned a quizzical smile on her. 'What's the matter, Olivia? Didn't you expect to find me here?'

Of course she hadn't! She'd expected him to be next door, tucked up on the sofa, sound asleep. 'I would have thought that was obvious!' she snapped back defensively at him. 'I don't make a habit of parading around half-naked in front of men I scarcely know!'

Through the indignation in her voice ran a nervous tremor of alarm. There was something about the way he was standing there—such a dark and powerfully potent male figure—that she found at once both menacing and faintly, intriguingly compelling.

He seemed to pick up the ambivalence in her as he stepped towards her with a smile. 'No need to be so nervous, Olivia.' His hand was on her arm, his voice a deep purr, as, moving still closer, he assured her, 'We can take this whole thing just as slow and easy as you wish.'

'What whole thing?' She swallowed drily, her heart hammering wildly, her limbs suddenly frozen. 'What are you talking about?'

'This.'

All at once, the hand on her arm had slipped round softly to encompass her waist, and with only the lightest of pressure, it seemed, he was drawing her weightlessly into his arms.

Olivia gasped soundlessly as the warmth of his body made contact with her own, the raw, burning heat of that rugged male torso and the firm, hard pressure of his hips and thighs sending garbled sensations of horror laced with excitement coursing through her veins. Then his free hand reached up to sweep through her hair, sending hot and cold shivers across her scalp, and she had no strength to snatch her head away as his lips began their slow descent towards hers.

There was no way that Olivia had been prepared for this development at all. Momentarily stunned and shocked, she stood immobile in his arms as firm, hard, sensuous lips claimed hers in a searing hot kiss. She was equally unprepared for the sudden shaft of sheer carnal intoxication that went surging through her, right down to her toes. As though someone had connected her up to a generator and switched on all the power.

She shivered, her limbs turned to water as he pulled her closer still, his mouth moving magically against hers, seducing her senses as he deepened his kiss. And a fire stole across her quivering flesh as she felt the hand at her waist move round with tantalising intent to cup the full, firm swell of her breast, the strong, hard fingers softly moulding, sending tingles of wild excitement blistering across her naked nerve-ends.

It was like being possessed by some force beyond control. For a heady moment she seemed suspended, all powers of resistance paralysed within her, then the hand at her breast began to move downwards, tugging at the towelling belt at her waist, and renewed fear and panic obliterated all other emotions as she felt it suddenly drop loose.

In an instant the power returned to her limbs and the will to resist was unclogging her brain. With a sudden, ferocious burst of strength, she hauled herself free from his embrace, her hands clutching at the dishevelled front of her robe as she staggered backwards, her eyes spitting fierce outrage.

'What the hell do you think you're doing?' she demanded furiously.

For a moment, Matthew didn't move. Slowly he narrowed his eyes at her, and when he spoke his voice was gritty and low. 'What the hell do you think I was doing? I was making love to my wife.'

'Oh, no . . .' She continued to back away from him, though he had made no move to close the gap. 'You can forget about anything like that.' With fumbling fingers she pulled her belt tight. 'That was never a part of our deal.'

Hard hazel eyes seemed to pierce right through her. 'Who says?' he demanded roughly.

Olivia was backed against the wall, hate and adrenalin surging through her, her every instinct poised for a fight. 'I say,' she informed him through clenched teeth. 'You're going against the deal we made. We agreed that our relationship was to be strictly business.'

'Did we?' One contemptuous dark eyebrow arched in riposte. 'We made a business deal, I'll grant you that, but I don't recall at any stage the content of our relationship being discussed. Am I wrong? Did you at any point stipulate that our marriage should be anything less than a full and properly consummated union?'

Olivia was gagging inwardly as he took a step forward to close the gap between them. 'I didn't think that was necessary,' she told him tightly, her face grown pale. 'I was under the impression that both of us were civilised people.'

'Then you were wrong.' He paused to look down at her, eyes like flints, and his tone was spiked with steel as he warned her, 'If you think I have any intention of enduring six months of celibacy, then I'm greatly afraid that you're in for a shock. You and I, my dear Olivia, are legally married, husband and wife—and husband and wife is what we're going to be, take my word for it, in every respect.'

Olivia's brain was in a whirl, desperately groping for some way out. 'If it's just celibacy you're worried about, you needn't be,' she assured him hurriedly. 'You've got Celine. You don't need me. You're perfectly free to continue your affair.'

'Is that so?' His expression changed, a hint of wry amusement in the dark eyes now. 'For such a little puritan as yourself, that's a remarkably laid-back attitude.' Then the lines of his features darkened again. 'But one, alas, that I don't share. I'm afraid, my dear Olivia, adultery is not in my repertoire. There will be no affairs, not with Celine nor with any other woman. What do I need with other women when I already have a wife?'

'But—for heaven's sake——' Olivia could see that what he was saying he was saying in deadly earnest. Her back was jammed against the wall. She could hear the blood hammering in her ears. 'You may have a wife,' she glared at him, 'but there's only one way you'll ever get your way with me—and that's if you're prepared to drag me to your bed and rape me!'

Her melodramatic little outburst brought a faint smile to the finely sculpted lips. 'Sorry, Olivia,' he shot back with a sneer, 'but rape's not in my repertoire either. I prefer my women willing.' The dark eyes scanned her trembling form. 'And I'm a patient man. Up to a point,' he emphasised. 'I'm prepared to give you time to come round.'

Olivia eyed him with dislike. Such unbridled masculine arrogance, to assume that she would ever come round! 'In that case, you'll wait for ever,' she took pleasure in informing him.

But Matthew simply smiled again, thinly, without humour. 'I repeat—I'll give you time.' Then he dropped his shoulders in an abrupt, impatient sigh. 'In the meantime, I suggest we get some sleep—since there's nothing else on the agenda.' He glanced across at the big, waiting bed. 'If we keep to opposite ends, we should be able to get through the night.'

This had to be another joke. 'Surely you don't seriously expect us to share the same bed?'

He glanced back at her. 'I can see only one bed, so what's the alternative? Don't worry,' he gave a tired shrug, 'I'm sure I'll manage to keep my hands off you.'

Olivia straightened. 'That's out of the question.' Then she reminded him, 'There's a sofa next door.'

Indifferently, he shrugged again. 'That's up to you. If you prefer to sleep on the couch, you go ahead.'

Obviously he hadn't understood. 'But I thought you——' she began.

But of course he had understood perfectly. 'Sorry, Olivia, I'm afraid not.' The dark eyes taunted as he shook his head. 'I've never had much of a passion for sleeping on sofas, alas.'

Ungallant swine! She glared at him.

He merely smiled an unrepentant smile as he headed for the bathroom. Then he added insult to injury as he called over his shoulder, 'You'll probably find some spare blankets in the cupboard. And if you find the sofa too uncomfortable, you can always come through and share the bed with me.'

As the bathroom door closed behind him, Olivia swore beneath her breath. She would sooner sleep on a bed of nails than slip between the sheets with him! With a last, lingering glance at tht expanse of silken luxury, she helped herself to an armful of blankets before retreating, vanquished, to the *salon* and the sofa.

What a naïve and trusting fool she'd been ever to have believed for a single moment that a man like Matthew Jordan would be capable of conducting this so-called marriage with decency and decorum! The next six months were going to be hell. Tonight, she sensed, was just the start.

From sheer exhaustion, Olivia slept, but she woke up next morning feeling as though she'd spent the entire night on the rack. Her neck ached, her back ached, her shoulders felt stiff. From head to toe she was a mass of cramps.

She staggered through to the bathroom to find Matthew already up and dressed and barking out a string of commands over the bedside telephone. So, even on his honeymoon, it was business as usual, she thought with a wry smile to herself as he barely bothered to glance her way. Thank heavens she hadn't been the least bit tempted to succumb to his sexual advances last night. If she had, she could just imagine how cheap and tacky she would be feeling now as, his carnal appetites temporarily appeased, he blithely set matrimonial matters aside to concentrate on Jordan Electronics. Wasn't he just a copy of her father!

He was still on the phone when she re-emerged from the bathroom, but again he failed to acknowledge her presence as she quickly grabbed some things from the wardrobe and hurried back to the *salon* to dress. It was only when he joined her downstairs for breakfast, three-quarters of an hour later, that he tossed her a casual, 'Good morning,' followed by a wicked, 'How did you sleep?'

'Like a log,' Olivia lied. He was already looking far too pleased with himself, without her presenting him with a gratuitous opportunity to gloat!

He was dressed more casually today in a blue-flecked tweed jacket and mid-grey trousers, his plain white shirt open at the neck, making Olivia feel just a little austere in her black wool skirt and matching cashmere cape.

'In that case,' he told her, quite clearly not believing a word, 'you'll be feeling anxious to get started with the day. I thought we could start off with a bit of sightseeing. Notre-Dame, that sort of thing.'

Olivia eyed him across the table. 'If you have business to attend to, please don't feel the need to interrupt it in order to entertain me. I can quite happily look after myself.' The truth was that nothing would suit her better than to be left in peace to her own devices.

But Matthew, for his own perverse reasons, was quite clearly not disposed to oblige. 'How could I possibly allow my darling bride of just one day to go wandering the streets of Paris alone?' The caustic humour in his eyes belied the note of mock-concern in his voice. 'Besides,' he insisted, still mocking, 'with a desirable young woman like you to distract him, how could a man even think of work?'

As he said it, he held her eyes and paused to stretch his long legs out under the table, causing Olivia to snatch hers away. Idiot, she chided herself, drinking her black coffee and avoiding his eyes. They were sitting in the middle of the hotel's crowded breakfast-room, yet he still had this disconcerting ability to make her feel threatened and vulnerable somehow.

'If you insist,' she answered drily, keeping her eyes fixed on the tablecloth. At least it was a relief to hear that he planned to spend the day away from the hotel. Away from the bedroom specifically. If they had to spend time together at all, the more of it that was spent out and about, the better. She was unlikely to get into any situations she couldn't handle in the middle of the Champs Elysées!

The morning, to her quiet astonishment, in fact went off remarkably well. Olivia was feeling much more relaxed, if a trifle footsore from tramping round the sights, when a taxi dropped them off at a little restaurant, well off the beaten track, for lunch.

It was one of Matthew's favourites, he had told her, a small, family-run place, all traditional check tablecloths, sturdy glass tumblers and plain white workaday plates. But the food more than justified the clutch of Michelin stars proudly displayed on the outside door. As Olivia finished off a rack of lamb that was one of the most delicious things she had ever tasted, she glanced across at her companion with a sudden twinge of curiosity.

'You know Paris well, don't you?' she put to him. In the course of the morning that had become very clear. He knew his way around the city almost like a native, and was full of those little gems of information that the guide-books never told you.

He helped himself to another portion of *dauphine* potatoes and smiled back at her mysteriously. 'I spent a lot of time in Paris in my youth. My parents lived here for a while. My father was a musician. He taught at the Paris Conservatoire.'

Olivia blinked at him in disbelief. 'A musician? Your father?' She could not have been more astounded if he had told her he was the son of the Pope.

'What's the matter?' he challenged with a smile. 'Did you think we Jordans knew nothing about anything except electronics?'

That was precisely what she had thought. A family of single-minded, money-making robots was how she had labelled them in her mind. 'No doubt you were never tempted to follow in your father's artistic footsteps,' she observed with a touch of acid in her voice. She might have been off target in her judgement of his family, but she had him sized up accurately, she was sure.

'I was never good enough to consider music as a career—and besides, if I'm honest, I was always more drawn to the world of computers. Unlike you,' he added, unmasking her, but without the faintest trace of condescension, 'I have a temperament more suited to business than to art.' He smiled as she glanced away. 'However, I do still play a bit, for my own amusement.'

The mind boggled. 'What do you play?'

'Piano, mostly. A bit of guitar.' He smiled at her bemused expression. 'Don't you believe me? I'll play something for you, if you like. There's a piano back at the hotel.'

'That won't be necessary,' she assured him tautly, suddenly anxious at the mention of the hotel. And equally anxious, too, at the sudden strange intimacy between them. Deliberately, she glanced away. She did not want to know Matthew Jordan's secrets, nor to be subjected to glimpses of his private life. She did not want to know anything about him. All she wanted was to keep him at a distance. At as great a distance as possible.

However, she needn't have worried. He seemed no more intent on divulging further secrets than she was on sharing them. He took a mouthful of his wine and told her with a provocative smile, 'While we're on the subject of things artistic . . . I've booked us a table at the Lido tonight.'

Olivia curled her nose in distaste. 'How nice!' she responded, her tone barbed with irony.

'I hope you've brought something suitable to wear.'

She threw him a crushing look. 'Do you mean, did I bring along my topless evening dress? No, I'm afraid I didn't.'

He smiled at that. 'Don't worry, my dear. Only the girls on stage are topless, not the audience.'

She smiled back sarcastically. 'Well, that's a relief.'

'It may be to you.' He held her eyes, his expression ambiguous, bringing a faint flush to her cheeks, before adding on a more serious note, 'So, did you bring along something suitable for such a sophisticated night out? Those prim little outfits you favour so much, I promise you, just won't do at all.'

Prim little outfits! She glared at him. He made her sound, sartorially, like a Women's Institute volunteer! Stung, she straightened defensively in her seat. 'I'm sorry that my taste in clothes is a little too restrained for you.' An image of the blonde Celine in the striking scarlet outfit she had worn to the wedding flashed unsummoned across her mind. 'No doubt you prefer something a little more showy.' And more vulgar, she elaborated to herself.

Matthew held her eyes. 'I'll show you what I like.' With a cool smile, he beckoned to the waiter.

'But let's have coffee first.'

He had the gleam in his eye of a man responding to a challenge, Olivia thought, as they left the little restaurant about half an hour later and climbed into a taxi. 'Rue du Faubourg-St-Honoré,' she heard him instruct the driver, and her heart gave an excited little squeeze as she recognised the name of possibly the most exclusive fashion street in Paris.

Nor were they merely window-shopping, she soon discovered as Matthew bade the cab driver draw up outside a particularly well-heeled establishment, then, as soon as he had paid the fare, took her firmly by the arm and proceeded to drag her inside.

Olivia gulped and protested weakly. In spite of his blanket condemnation of her wardrobe, she prided herself on dressing well, if somewhat conservatively. She had even been known to indulge in the occasional extravagance. But this was in another league. Without even looking at the price tags, just by the smell of the place, she could tell that one of their leather belts probably cost the equivalent of what she would spend on a winter coat.

A salesperson with that immaculate brand of chic and grooming that only the French knew how to achieve had appeared apparently out of nowhere and was bearing down on them with a predatory smile. '*Bonjour, madame, monsieur,*' she intoned. '*Puis-je vous être de service?*' Can I help you?

'I want something special for my wife,' Olivia

heard Matthew explain in faultless French.
'Something for evening. Semi-formal.'

'*Bien.*' The woman turned to Olivia with an
appraising smile. '*Venez ici,*' she invited, and
proceeded to lead her dumbstruck client to the
other end of the shop, where a rail of
monumentally expensive-looking silk dresses
hung. Perfectly manicured red fingernails ran
along the contents of the rail, then paused to pick
out a green silk taffeta creation which was
promptly held up for *madame's* approval.

From what Olivia could make out, it had a
neckline that went plunging right down to the
midriff and a slit up the side from knee to thigh.
She shook her head. 'I don't think so,' she said,
adding with heavy irony for the benefit of
Matthew, who was hovering at her side, 'Green's
not really my colour, I'm afraid.'

The woman turned to study the rail some more,
but before she could lay hands on some other
scandalous concoction Olivia stepped forward and
made her own choice. 'I like this one, she said,
pointing to a black crêpe tube with just a sprinkling
of diamanté on the shoulders.

But before the assistant's fingers had time to
reach for the hanger, Matthew cut in. '*Pas noir,*' he
decreed autocratically. 'No black. That's my only
reservation.'

Olivia made a face. 'But I like black!'

'And you already have a wardrobeful.' Before
she could argue further, he leaned forward
decisively and picked a dress from off the rail.
'This one,' he declared, holding aloft an eye-

catching cerise creation that Olivia would never normally have dared to consider.

The sales assistant smiled her approval—'*Parfait, monsieur!*'—as Matthew thrust the garment at Olivia. 'Try it on,' he commanded. 'I want to see how it looks.'

A few minutes later, in the privacy of the dressing-room, Olivia had to admit that it looked quite stunning. It was high at the front and low at the back, and it fitted her like a second skin. She smiled at her reflection in the mirror, but inwardly she was shaking her head. It was an exquisite dress, no doubt about that, but with its slinky, almost vampish cut it definitely wasn't her. Even Matthew would realise that the moment he set eyes on her.

'*Quelle merveille!*' The sales assistant virtually applauded as Olivia stepped out self-consciously from behind the dressing-room curtain. And Matthew proved himself equally undiscerning. 'Terrific! We'll take it,' he responded at once.

Olivia stared at him, aghast. 'But it's not my type of thing!' she protested. 'I couldn't possibly appear in public in a dress like this!'

'Nonsense! You can and you will. You look absolutely ravishing, my dear.' Then, overriding her feeble dissent, he bundled into her unwilling arms a pile of carefully selected hangers bearing an assortment of elegant day dresses, stylish skirts and jewel-coloured blouses. 'Now try these on,' he commanded. 'I'm not through with you yet.'

Olivia was seething as she disappeared behind the curtain again. Who did the damned man think he was, taking her over like this? She sifted resentfully through the hangers, searching in vain for something with a familiar cut to it, something she knew she would feel comfortable in, yet knowing it didn't matter a damn whether his choice had her approval or not. He would doubtless insist on satisfying his male vanity by buying what he had picked out anyway.

Well, let him throw away his money if he liked! She would do likewise with the clothes as soon as she was free of him.

She was right about him insisting on buying the lot—with one small concession to her own expressed preference. 'Since you've been such a very good girl,' he told her with a twist at the end of the marathon, 'I'll allow you to have the black as well.' And, as, laden with parcels, they climbed into a taxi and headed back to the hotel, he informed her with a malicious grin, 'Now you're ready for Paris. And for life as Mrs Matthew Jordan.'

For the latter she would never be ready, Olivia confided privately to herself. But for Paris, who knew? With sceptical interest at her own transformation, she regarded her reflection in the sitting-room mirror later that night, as she got ready to go out.

She had tried on the black dress first, having reluctantly conceded that none of her own things would fit the bill, and knowing that at least in black she always felt comfortable. But something had drawn her towards the cerise, the slinky little number that had been Matthew's first choice, and for some outlandish reason, totally inexplicable, even to herself, she had decided to stick with it. The whole situation's crazy, she told herself. I may as well act crazy too.

Out of habit, she had pinned her hair in a neat chignon, but it looked wrong somehow. She studied herself in the mirror. The dramatic colour and lines of the dress demanded a more dramatic hairstyle as well. Deftly she twisted her shiny dark tresses into a high topknot, then added the big, bold ear-rings that the woman in the shop had picked out for her. That looked better. She made a face. Well, at least it looked different.

Matthew's approval was less ambivalent as, with a discreet tap on the door, he came into the room. 'The duckling has turned into a swan,' he pronounced, coming to stand alongside her in front of the mirror.

He was dressed in a slim dark suit, white shirt and burgundy tie, his dark hair glistening, his tanned, handsome features relaxed and smiling as he came to drape her new silk shawl about her shoulders. He looks like every girl's dream escort, Olivia couldn't help thinking to herself, aware of a strange, unsettling new feeling somewhere in the pit of her stomach. It was almost a pity, she decided, that he was nothing but an unscrupulous sham underneath.

It was to be as much an evening of revelations as the day itself had been.

The Lido was nothing like Olivia had expected. No sleazy nightclub this, and certainly no sleazy clientele. The tiered rows of tables in a hall as big as the London Palladium were packed with elegant, well-dressed couples. An air of opulence and good taste prevailed. She was suddenly immensely glad of her new dress. Anything less glamorous would have appeared dowdy—and she had to confess to a secret pleasure in the sensuous, ultra-feminine way it made her feel.

The show itself was a million light years away from the nasty little strip-show she had been half dreading. A mixture of the Folies Bergère and Busby Berkeley, it was a veritable feast for the eyes. As the stage exploded in a riot of colour, with each scene more spectacular than the one before it, Olivia sat mesmerised, drinking in every magic minute. Never in her life before had she seen anything quite like it. Not for a long time had she enjoyed herself so much.

'Well, was that so decadent?' Matthew enquired with a smile as the final curtain came down and they sat drinking a last cup of coffee.

Olivia was on the point of answering, 'It wasn't really decadent at all,' while simultaneously acknowledging to herself that she really ought to have known all along that Matthew Jordan was not the type of tasteless man who would subject a woman to some spectacle that she might find offensive. But, for some perverse reason, she answered instead, 'Do you take all your girlfriends to the Lido?'

'You're not my girlfriend. You're my wife.'

'Not in any real sense, thank goodness.'

'That's true. At least, for the moment.' As his eyes locked with hers, their expression grew hard, no trace of the warmth and friendliness of before. 'But situations,' he warned, 'can change.'

'Not this one,' Olivia assured him harshly, responding to the change of mood. Then she added maliciously, just for good measure, 'So, just in case you were hoping that by bringing me to see this erotic little show you might manage to get me in the mood to succumb to your sexual advances, I'm sorry to tell you you've wasted your time!'

Even as she was saying it, she felt faintly ashamed. For, in her heart, she knew perfectly well that such a gauche seduction was not his style at all. And all at once, for no reason at all, a perfectly pleasant evening had been spoiled.

In the taxi on the way back to the hotel the two of them exchanged not a word, though Olivia was aware, from time to time, of glittering dark eyes fixed on her face. In angry silence they took the lift up to their suite—and it was only once they were safely in the privacy of their own rooms that Matthew finally retaliated.

As, without a backward glance, she proceeded to head for the sitting-room door, he reached out and grabbed her by the arm, pulling her to him in a brutal embrace.

'Just a minute,' he snarled. 'You forgot to say goodnight.' And the deep, dark eyes with their thick, black lashes burned down threateningly into hers as he went on, contemptuously mimicking her earlier outburst at the club, 'That erotic little show may have failed to get my prim little wife in the mood, but it sure as hell worked wonders for me!'

Then he was jerking her helpless body against his

as his mouth ground down in a punishing kiss, strong fingers clamped against the back of her skull, making it useless for her to resist. Without preamble, his free hand moved round to administer a rough caress to her breast, probing the thin silk of her dress, sending hot, humiliating shafts through her veins.

Olivia was gasping for breath as he devoured her roughly with his hands and his lips, her limbs trembling from the force of his assault as he paused to demand in a harsh, roughened voice, 'So, my darling little wife, will you be sharing your husband's bed tonight?'

In panic and fury, Olivia drew back. 'Never!' she spat at him in vicious response.

Still he held her, his fingers cruel steel, his eyes like lances as he cuttingly informed her, 'Then perhaps you should consider the fact that you're not the only one who can renege on a deal. Since you refuse to be my wife in any real sense, it's equally within my power to refuse to go ahead with my side of the bargain!'

As roughly as he had grabbed her, he released her now and pushed her bodily towards the *salon* door. 'Perhaps you ought to think about that while you're lying next door on the sofa protecting your precious cold-blooded virtue!'

CHAPTER SIX

IT WAS a deeply troubled Olivia who crawled beneath the blankets on the sofa that night. What the hell had she got herself into? And what exactly had Matthew meant by that threat?

At the time she hadn't hung around to enquire. Her lips bruised and burning from his humiliating assault, she had staggered gratefully through the *salon* doorway, slammed the door shut and turned the key in the lock. But throughout the night, as she tossed and turned, one question was burning in her brain. Surely Matthew hadn't been serious about reneging on their deal? Surely she hadn't locked herself into six months of purgatory to emerge empty-handed at the end of it all?

She had her answer the following morning.

Matthew threw her a glacial look when she demanded, tight-lipped, that he explain immediately what he had meant. 'Very simple, my dear Olivia.' The dark hazel eyes were steely hard as in answer he strode over to the bedside phone, lifted the receiver and dialled the operator. 'Get me this number in England, please,' he said in clear and careful French, so that Olivia understood every word. Then he proceeded to reel off the number of Jordan Electronics.

As they waited in silence for the operator to call back, he sat on the edge of the unmade bed, a dark, hostile figure in a light grey suit, his eyes never leaving Olivia's face. She stood like a nervous wraith near the doorway, hating him with every atom of her strength.

As the phone began to shrill, he picked it up. 'Put me through to the Legal Department.' Then, a moment later, after a perfunctory exchange of pleasantries . . . 'Those transfer papers you were working on for Garland's—put them on hold. Indefinitely,' he commanded.

He laid down the phone and stood up slowly. '*That*,' he said harshly, 'is what I meant.'

So it was precisely as she had feared. Olivia was close to tears. Half pleadingly, she looked at him. 'But you can't do that,' she protested feebly, her heart as tight as a drum in her chest. 'You signed a legal agreement that you would hand over Garland's to me after we were married!'

Matthew demolished her with a look. 'An agreement which is not worth the paper it's written on should I decide to have the marriage annulled.' He paused, then proceeded on a note of menace, 'And an annulment, in the circumstances, wouldn't be difficult to obtain.'

That was something she had not thought of. Olivia felt herself go pale. 'Surely you can't be serious!' she wailed.

Matthew's eyebrows lifted in a silent indictment. 'Why not?' he demanded. 'You appear to be.'

'But that's different!' she protested. 'How can you possibly compare my objections to . . . the sort of intimacies you seem to expect . . . with this totally wilful decision on your part to break your side of the bargain? Surely even you can see there's a world of difference between the two?'

He smiled unkindly. 'I'm afraid I don't. All I can see is that you don't seem to like being forced to take a taste of your own medicine for a change. Well, that's too bad, my dear Olivia.' His tone was mocking as he went on, 'I believe in giving as good as I get. I'm afraid I'm not the soft touch you seemed to suppose.'

Soft touch! If she had been feeling less crushed, she might have laughed. She doubted that even his mother had ever thought of him as that!

She glared across at him in helpless anger. He was being totally unreasonable and there appeared to be little point in arguing. Totally deflated, she demanded, 'So where do you suggest we go from here?'

He smiled without humour, the dark eyes intransigent, as he came round the bed and stood before her. 'Where we go, I would suggest, is up to you. As I told you before, I'm a patient man—though my patience is far from boundless, and already it's starting to wear a bit thin . . .'

As he raked her stunned and miserable form with those ruthlessly calculating eyes, Olivia suddenly felt herself tense—and burned with the memory of last night's assault. But then, dismissively, he turned away. 'In the meantime, where *I'm* going is downstairs to have breakfast. Suit yourself whether you join me or not.'

That angry and bitter exchange more or less set the emotional tone of their relationship over the days that followed. The hours they spent alone together in the confines of the hotel were brittle and uneasy—and made all the more uncomfortable, somehow, by the faintly incongruous fact that when they were away from the hotel they actually got on surprisingly well.

When he wasn't being his usual overbearing, autocratic self, Matthew, Olivia was discovering, could be thoroughly agreeable and entertaining company. And it wasn't simply because he knew Paris so well and had such a fund of stories to tell. There was an easygoing side to him that made relaxing with him easy. She was even beginning to appreciate his quirky, irreverent sense of humour.

It was almost a pity, she found herself thinking, that they'd been forced into this ridiculous marriage. In other, less unnatural circumstances, it might have been possible for them to be friends.

But only *might*, for he could change like the wind—as he roundly demonstrated one afternoon.

As they window-shopped after an amiable lunch, he paused to gaze at the seductive display in the window of a high-class lingerie shop. 'Which do you prefer, the black or the cream?' he enquired with a wicked smile, indicating two gossamer nighties and their matching *négligés*.

Instantly, an alarm bell started clamouring inside Olivia's head. 'They're both a bit too exotic for me,' she answered self-consciously.

'Yes, but if you had to choose, which do you

prefer?'

She hesitated, her cheeks suddenly burning. 'Well . . . the black, I suppose.'

The words were scarcely out of her mouth before he had disappeared inside the shop. Ten minutes later he re-emerged, carrying a lavishly gift-wrapped box. A devilish smile curled round his lips as he looked at her flushed, embarrassed face. 'Don't look so perturbed, *chérie*,' he admonished. 'Who said anything about this being for you?'

His words had thrown her, even shocked her slightly. So the gift, appropriately, was for Celine. A jumbled mixture of irritation and relief, disappointment and anger went flooding through her. How often, she wondered, even in Paris, did a husband enlist the assitance of his wife in choosing lingerie for his mistress —particularly when they were still on their honeymoon? And again she put up a prayer of thanks that she was continuing to stand absolutely firm on the issue of their sleeping arrangements.

That issue—like the threatened annulment —had never been raised again, though when they were alone in their suite together it hung between them like naked barbed wire. With any luck, Olivia was praying, Matthew would eventually come round to the fact that she was never going to change her mind—in spite of, or even partly *because* of this new threat he was dangling over her head. For there was no way she would agree to conceding sexual favours to win him round. She had already stooped low enough by agreeing, in the first place, to this marriage. But all the way down into the gutter she would never allow herself to go.

So all she could do now was pray that his sense of honour would win through. She would not push him, she decided, as long as he did not push her. And, though he was not a man who would easily concede defeat, he must surely eventually realise that this game he was playing was not worth the fight—and that the only decent thing to do was to honour the agreement that they had made.

In the meantime, the honeymoon was almost over, and for their very last evening together in Paris Matthew had booked a table on a *bâteau mouche*.

'It's a floating restaurant,' he had explained when she had asked, 'that wends its way up and down the Seine. I've never actually been on one myself, so it'll be a first for both of us.'

For the occasion Olivia had chosen to wear another exotic item from her new wardrobe—a sapphire blue two-piece, sculpted around the waist and hips, softly draped around the bust. And, once again, she had abandoned her unadventurous chignon in favour of the more chic, more flattering topknot.

As she and Matthew were shown to their table, she was aware of a number of eyes on them. Admiring eyes. And she smiled to herself. Even amid all the elegant examples of Parisian manhood who were present, there was no doubt that Matthew stood out. He had an easy, panther-like grace about him that, harnessed to his naturally striking good looks, added up to the sort of man who quite unselfconsciously turned women's heads.

She watched him out of the corner of her eye and walked tall, knowing that this evening at least she was a match for him. Then, as she sat down opposite him at the table, she glanced round with a confident smile. Quite unaccountably, her spirits were high.

Matthew ordered champagne and they drank a toast before the meal began. 'To Paris!' Matthew proposed. Then, as Olivia raised her glass to endorse the sentiment, he added with a twinkle in his eye, 'You should visit it more often. It appears to agree with you.'

She drank and watched him over the rim of her glass. 'And what exactly do you mean by that?'

'I mean that I see before me a totally transformed Olivia. Whatever happened to the mousy little madam who arrived here with me just six days ago?'

Olivia felt her cheeks flush slightly. Mousy little madam, indeed! Was that really the impression she had given? Instantly she felt her defences leap up as, in a faintly clipped voice, she assured him, 'It's only a borrowed dress and a temporary new hairdo. Underneath this exotic new plumage, I'm still just as mousy as before.'

He smiled and brushed away the denial. 'I'm not talking about the plumage, I'm talking about the light in your eye. I'm talking about your smile and the way your whole personality has suddenly unclenched itself.'

Olivia laughed at the description. 'And you think Paris has something to do with it?'

'Well, something's done it, that's for sure.' For a moment, the dark hazel eyes held hers, seeming to probe right down to her soul. 'If not Paris, then what?' he asked.

There was nothing else it could be, yet, in sudden discomfort, she lowered her eyes.

Matthew was still watching her. 'Whatever's responsible, it suits you. I must say I like this Olivia a whole lot better than the other one.'

'Oh?' She glanced up and caught the flash of humour in his eyes. 'And what was so wrong with the other one, I'd like to know?'

'Simple.' He sat back, leaning broad shoulders against the back of his chair as he continued, minutely, to survey her. 'This one's a woman. The other one wasn't.'

'Oh, and what was she?' There was a slight sting in her voice again. 'Was she, perhaps, a man?'

'No, no, she was never a man. But she was only half a woman.' He paused, the dark eyes probing like lasers. 'For some reason, she was struggling to turn herself into that sexless object, a businesswoman.'

There was more than a touch of chauvinism in that remark, it occurred to Olivia. She narrowed her eyes and leaned towards him, moving from defence to attack. 'And why should a businesswoman be considered sexless in your book? You describe yourself as a businessman. I'm sure you don't consider that that makes you any less of a man?'

He held her eyes. 'I'm a businessman from nine to five, but twenty-four hours a day I'm a man. That's where we differed, Olivia. When I first met you you seemed determined to submerge your entire identity beneath that businesswoman façade.' His gaze brushed the contours of her face, softly, like a caress. 'I don't know what it was supposed to be protecting you from, but I prefer you with your armour off.'

Suddenly, for her part, Olivia was half wishing she had kept it on. This far too accurate analysis of her secret self had brought a flame to her face and a flutter to her heart. She felt exposed, dissected, all her wordly weaknesses revealed. She was relieved as a waiter came alongside them and handed a menu to each of them in turn.

As the man moved off, Matthew leaned across the table. 'Relax, Olivia,' he urged. 'I think we've peeled off enough layers for the moment.' Then he smiled at her devilishly and threw her a wink. 'But I warn you, the night is still young!'

The night, however, proceeded to unfold without a hitch. It was as though they were both making an unconscious effort to end their Parisian sojourn on an agreeable note.

And there was a surprise in store . . .

It was just as they were finishing dessert that suddenly a female voice called out, 'Matthew! I

knew it was you!' And the next instant an
elegantly dressed woman about Matthew's own
age was standing alongside them, smiling
broadly.

As Matthew glanced up at her, his own face
broke into a smile. 'Chantal!' he exclaimed,
rising to his feet. 'How wonderful to see you!'

As they embraced like old friends and
exchanged warm kisses, Olivia had to fight
down a strange new sensation that suddenly
twisted at her insides. She knew it could not be
jealousy, but it felt remarkably similar.

Then Matthew was turning away from the
woman and towards Olivia once again. 'Chantal,
I want you to meet someone very special. This is
Olivia, my new wife.'

'Wife?' The woman's eyes widened with
surprise and delight as Olivia rose to offer her
hand. 'But she's absolutely lovely!' she
exclaimed. 'Matthew, you wicked boy, why
didn't you tell us you were married?'

Olivia watched with oddly mixed feelings as,
without a stutter or a pause, he slipped instantly
into the act he performed so well. If she hadn't
known the cold, hard truth, even she might
easily have mistaken him for a lovestruck newly-
wed. 'It all happened very suddenly. And very
recently. As a matter of fact, Olivia and I are here
in Paris on our honeymoon.'

Chantal beamed with doubled delight. 'You
must come at once and tell Pierre—both of you.'
She took Olivia's arm. 'We're down there at the
other end with a couple of Pierre's clients from

the States. Join us for coffee,' she almost pleaded, tugging gently at Matthew's lapel. 'I know the two of you would rather be alone, but it's been so long, and Pierre would love to see you.'

There was nothing to do but succumb to her pleas, and the next three-quarters of an hour were spent in the affectionate, ebullient company of Chantal and Pierre and their American friends.

'I knew Matthew when he was twelve years old,' Chantal confided with a giggle to Olivia. 'He was horrible!' She curled up her nose. 'All skinned knees and frogs in his pockets and nasty schoolboy tricks.' Then she sighed and winked playfully across at her husband as she added, a note of mischief in her voice, 'If I'd known how he was going to turn out, I might have tried a little harder to make him fall in love with me.'

Matthew grinned across at her. 'You're far too modest, Chantal. You know perfectly well I was always in love with you.'

'Hah!' the Frenchwoman scoffed, and turned to Olivia. 'Pay no attention to him! I was never his type—too much of a tomboy. He always preferred the gentler, more refined and feminine types. Like yourself,' she added admiringly. 'You're exactly the kind of girl I always knew Matthew would end up marrying.'

'She knows me so well.' Matthew held Olivia's eyes, the doting husband, play-acting again, and Olivia couldn't resist observing, in an equally doting tone of voice,

'He's such an utterly shameless charmer. Was he that bad as a little boy?'

Chantal laughed, delighted, and wagged her finger across the table at Matthew. 'She's got you sized up, I see!' Then, to Olivia, 'I'm afraid he always was a shameless charmer.' She smiled an almost solemn smile. 'You're a lucky girl, you know.'

They returned to their own table for brandy and liqueurs, having promised faithfully that next time they were in Paris they would have dinner with Chantal and Pierre. Olivia sipped her green Chartreuse, feeling faintly regretful that the promise would never be kept. They were nice people. She would have rather enjoyed meeting them again.

But for now she was strangely, secretly pleased to have Matthew all to herself again.

A small dance band had started playing and several couples had left their tables and made their way on to the floor. Feeling pleasantly mellow and relaxed, Olivia turned for a moment to watch, a happy smile on her lips, feet tapping cheerfully in time to the music.

Matthew's eyes were on her. 'Shall we?' he invited, reading her mood, and she nodded, glad that he had asked. Suddenly she was in the mood for dancing. With a flush of excitement she got to her feet.

He danced well, as she had known he would, his movements natural and fluid as he guided her across the floor, the pressure of his hand against her waist firm and sure, yet soft as a whisper. The long, lean fingers clasping her own felt hard and strong, yet their grip was light, and the brush of the broad chest against her breasts was warm and not at all unpleasant. She felt not a glimmer of an urge to draw away as his chin leaned softly against her cheek. She closed her eyes and drifted with the music, aware that her senses were suddenly singing. It was true what he had said earlier about Paris. It was doing magical things to her.

At the end of that first dance, they danced some more. And then they danced some more again. But all too soon the music ended and the *bateau mouche* was docking at the quayside.

As Matthew escorted her ashore, one hand still lightly around her waist, Olivia half heard herself complain, 'What a pity we have to go back. I could have danced all night.'

He was smiling down at her. 'Then there's no reason why you can't. There are plenty of nightclubs we can go on to if you'd rather not go back to the hotel just yet.'

'But we have to get up so early tomorrow to catch our wretched flight back home.' She sighed despondently as he hailed a cab. 'I suppose we'd better not.'

'We could always have a private little party of our own, back at the hotel,' Matthew suggested as the cab drew up alongside them and they climbed inside.

Olivia glanced up to meet his eyes. The proposition had a pleasing ring. 'OK, you're on!' she agreed with a smile, not objecting in the least to the arm that was slipping around her, drawing her close. With a sigh, she dropped her head against his shoulder, enjoying his companionable warmth. It had been such a very special evening, she didn't want it to end just yet.

Back at their suite, as she kicked off her shoes, Matthew rang down to room service for a bottle of champagne while she fiddled with the radio till she found some suitable late-night music.

'So, where's the party going to be? Your room or mine?' asked Matthew with a smile.

'Mine.' She caught him by the hand and led him through to the *salon*. 'There's much more room to dance in mine,' she added in a playful, teasing tone.

With her shoes off, she discovered, she reached barely to his broad, male shoulders, and she seemed almost to be floating in the sure, strong grip of his arms as they moved in slow time to the music. It was a dizzy, dreamlike feeling, more ethereal than real, as she laid her cheek against the wide expanse of chest, one hand resting lightly on his shoulder while the the other balanced a half-full glass of bubbly.

Matthew breath was soft against her hair as he questioned, with a light smile in his voice, 'How on earth can you drink and dance at the same time, I'd like to know?'

'Easy.' She giggled and took a mouthful, then held the glass up to his lips. 'Go on, try for yourself,' she urged. 'Help me finish it.'

He drank, humouring her, then let his dark eyes roam her face as she drained the last few drops herself and sighed contentedly, letting her weight fall against him, loving the warm, safe feel of his arms.

Olivia was deliciously aware of the hand that had begun to caress her back and now was slowly moving upwards to massage the sensitive nape of her neck. She moaned slightly, instinctively pressing into the caress, and let her eyes close dreamily as long, strong, gentle fingers slid onwards on their sensuous journey, delicately smoothing her upswept hair.

The next instant, before she had realised what he was up to, he had removed the combs that held her topknot in place. With a soft, silky swish, her long, dark hair fell in a soft cloud around her ears. Then his fingers were trailing through the loose silken tresses, sending quicksilver shafts of breathless sensation licking like hot flames across her scalp.

'Naughty!' Half mesmerised by this heady sensation that was sweeping like a warm tide through her veins, Olivia leaned her head back a little from his chest and squinted up into hypnotic hazel eyes. 'Now you've completely ruined my hairdo,' she chided, feeling a stab of longing pierce right through her as she met the smouldering dark gaze. Suddenly, the state of her coiffure was the very last thing on her mind.

The burning eyes smiled down, unrepentant. 'I already told you, I prefer it like this.' Then his fingers lightly caught her chin and he was gazing down into her face, seeming to explore her very soul with those deeply penetrating, bright dark eyes.

For one long, endless moment, Olivia hung suspended—waiting, knowing what would happen next, and longing for it with every atom of her being. Her breath had frozen in her breast, her lips lightly parted in anticipation, and the invitation in her deep blue eyes shone as clear as neon in her flushed, excited face.

And it seemed she would expire from the agony of the moment, her poor heart clamouring so hard that its anguish seemed to fill the room, until, at last, the hand at her waist was crushing her body against his and his lips came down to conquer hers in a fierce and hungrily compelling kiss.

It was a kiss she would remember and relive many times in the weeks ahead. Like a bush fire tearing through her senses, devouring, ripping her apart.

She could feel his desire, hot and strong, as his hard male body pressed against hers. But beyond that raw power burned a richly smouldering, carefully controlled sensuality. And it was to this deep, erotic, secret promise that she could feel her flesh responding, as it licked into life a longing in her that she had never known before.

As Matthew's lips ground down on hers, his moist tongue exploring the inner sweetness of her mouth, Olivia felt her arms twine round his neck and was dimly aware of the empty champagne glass falling with a soft thud to the carpeted floor. Then her pulses quickened and she shivered, weak with wanting, as his hand came round to cup her breast. All at once her senses were in turmoil, a bubbling, boiling, sweet agony of desire as, with one expert hand, he circled and caressed, while the other swiftly began to undo the row of buttons at the back of her blouse.

'Olivia, Olivia . . .'

As the slippery silk back of the blouse fell open and his fingers made contact with her naked flesh, Olivia felt a ripple of excitement burning like wildfire down her spine. Helplessly, she gasped and let out a little moan. Then he was peeling the thin silk from her shoulders, his lips bending to press a trail of molten hot kisses across her shivering, defenceless flesh.

One movement and the blouse had slithered forward, exposing her eager, uptilted breasts. Then, as it fell to the floor with a whisper of surrender, suddenly he was gathering her into his arms.

'I think we should continue this next door,' he was murmuring huskily against her hair. Then he was carrying her through to the bedroom, and she was clinging to him, her senses reeling, her eyes closed tight, her heart beating like a drum.

He laid her down against the sheets, pausing to kiss her on the lips—but a gentle, seductive, lingering kiss, without the forceful urgency of before. Then, as he shed his shirt and tie and lay alongside her on the huge four-poster bed, he was drawing her gently into his arms, his hands caressing, his lips exploring, softly whispering her name.

He paused to peel away his own trousers and the restraining silk skirt she still wore, then gathered her to him again, his body warm and eager and hard. Then he was leaning across her, the dark eyes gazing down into her face as he cupped her ripe, swollen breasts in his palms, his thumbs caressing the taut, hardened nipples, sending shock-waves of excitement racing to her loins.

With growing hunger she pressed against him, her tentative, unschooled fingers responding to the rising need in her as they caressed with a mounting sense of wonder the firm, hard contours of the deeply muscled chest, the powerful, dark-tanned shoulders, the sinuously rippling back.

She could feel his heart hammering against her own as he rained fiery kisses across her throat, down her collarbone, over her shoulders, then sent shafts of raw electricity ricocheting through her as, with excruciating thoroughness, he paused to draw into his mouth the aching peak of each breast in turn.

Involuntarily she felt her back arch and the breath caught in her throat in a hungry moan. This can't be happening, her brain was shouting. This has to be a dream.

But it was no dream. As he lowered himself on top of her, one hand in her damp and tousled hair, the other was moving downwards to ease the lacy briefs away.

'Olivia, my lovely. Olivia, my wife . . .'

In that moment her entire body stiffened, sudden, cold panic stamping on the brakes. Was she mad? her brain was clamouring. Had she taken leave of her senses? She was on the brink of surrendering herself to a man for whom sex was no more than a commodity to be used as leverage in a business deal.

With the strength of harsh reason she struggled

free from his embrace. 'No! Let me go! Let me go this minute!'

His body was still pinning her to the bed. With a frown, he raised his head to look at her, but did not move away. 'Olivia, my love,' he started to soothe, 'don't be afraid. There's nothing to be afraid of.'

She struggled more fiercely, fists pummelling his shoulders and chest, sheer, unbridled fear filling her mouth with venom. 'You brute—let me go this minute! You bullying bastard! You filthy animal!'

Shock was written all over Matthew's face as he moved away then, instantly freeing her. And before he could say a word she was wriggling away from him, staggering to the floor, then fleeing like a hunted animal across the room and through the door into the safety of the *salon*.

As she turned to slam the door behind her, she caught a brief glimpse of stunned dark eyes boring into her. Then, with fumbling fingers, she was snapping the lock shut.

'Keep out, you animal! Leave me alone!' she sobbed helplessly beneath her breath. All at once her trembling legs seemed to buckle under her, and she sank weeping to the floor.

Some dark voice in the caverns of her soul was telling her what she already knew: that her cruel and bitter accusations were nothing but self-deceiving lies. And not all the locked doors in the world could keep her safe from him any more.

CHAPTER SEVEN

'HI, SIS! We're back!'

Olivia glanced up from her magazine as Richard came bounding into the sitting-room, his fair hair windblown, his wide blue eyes alight with youthful energy and enthusiasm. She smiled at him and rose from her chair. 'So how did the gliding lesson go?'

'Great! Matthew says next time we go up I can take the controls for a while.'

'Good for you!' Her eyebrows lifted with sisterly pride. 'I hope you're being an attentive pupil.'

'He's the brightest pupil I've ever had.' As Matthew came striding through the doorway, Olivia felt every muscle in her body go stiff. These days, just the sight of him was like a physical rebuke. He paused in the middle of the room, a tall, commanding figure in black cord trousers and matching black polo-neck sweater, and fixed her with piercing hazel eyes. 'You should have come along,' he told her. 'It was a beautiful day. You would have enjoyed yourself.'

Self-consciously Olivia glanced away, knowing that the remark had been made solely for her brother's benefit. Matthew was no more anxious to spend time in her company than she was to spend time in his. 'Perhaps some other time,' she responded quietly.

Then she had to keep a tight hold on her smile as

Richard elaborated brightly, 'You can come along and watch us this summer. Matthew says I can come and spend some of my summer vac here with you. I've even managed to twist his arm into agreeing to a skiing holiday next Christmas.'

Matthew reached out to tousle the boy's hair affectionately, deliberately catching Olivia's eye as he answered ambiguously, 'I said "maybe", remember? I didn't make any promises. A lot of things could happen between now and Christmas.'

Like a divorce—or, worse still, an annulment— Olivia thought grimly to herself, fighting the pang of guilt that shot through her at this deception she and Matthew were perpetrating. As long as it had involved just the two of them, the situation had been almost tolerable. But involving her teenage brother in this insidious web of lies was something her conscience was having trouble coming to terms with.

Unfortunately, the situation had been foisted on her. Just a matter of days ago, completely out of the blue, Richard had phoned her at St Albans.

'I was just wondering how my newly-married sister's getting on,' he'd begun. 'How's married life agreeing with you?'

It had been a lovely surprise to hear from him—their first communication, apart from the couple of unanswered letters she had sent him, since that somewhat taut exchange when she had called to tell him about her impending marriage. 'Everything's just fine with me,' she'd lied. 'Tell me about yourself. How are things with you?'

'Great, just great. I've got a half-term holiday

coming up this weekend . . .' He had paused for a moment before continuing, and his tone had been contrite as he'd gone on to tell her, 'I thought I might come and spend it with you—if you'll agree to have me, that is. I've decided maybe I was a bit hasty. I ought at least to meet this new husband of yours before I make up my mind about him. Even if he is a Jordan,' he'd added with a twist of humour. 'What do you say, Sis? Do you forgive me? Will you let me spend a long weekend at St Albans?'

'Of course! I'd be delighted to see you.' The sentiment was true, but she'd had reservations, all the same. She had hated falling out with Richard, and she was delighted that he was keen to make it up. But, at the same time, she had been secretly hoping that it might be possible to see out the six months of this wretched marriage without her brother becoming involved. This unexpected move on his part had totally put her on the spot. 'But don't feel you have to come rushing down here at your half-term if you've got better things to do. There's plenty of time for you to meet Matthew,' she had hedged.

But he'd obviously made up his mind. 'No, I want to come.' Then he'd added, misinterpreting her hesitation, 'Unless you don't want to see me, of course.'

That was the last thing she had wanted him to think! 'Idiot!' she'd protested straight away. 'Of course I want to see you, Richie! It's just that I thought you might have something more exciting lined up with your friends. I'm very glad to hear you don't.' On a warm note, she had reassured him, 'I'm going to get the spare room ready for you this very afternoon!'

As she had laid down the phone, she'd smiled wryly to herself. In this particular instance, getting the spare room ready would involve a little more than simply putting clean sheets on the bed. She would have to empty the cupboards and drawers and move out all her things.

For the past three weeks, since their return to England after that disastrous last night in Paris, Olivia had adopted the spare room as a kind of private sanctuary. Not only did she sleep there, with the door locked, at night, she also frequently retired to its peaceful seclusion with a book in the evenings with Matthew was at home. It was an arrangement, she suspected, that suited him as much as her.

She could tell he had not forgiven her for that brutal, insensitive verbal attack, and, in truth, she had not expected him to. For, despite her shame at what had passed the night, Olivia had never apologised.

The omission had been deliberate, the only way that she could see of coping with the maelstrom of conflicting emotions that were suddenly besieging her.

Predominant among these emotions was fear. Once, Olivia had believed that she was capable of total self-control in certain matters. It had come as a devastating shock to discover that she was not. That night in Paris, she had reacted to Matthew as any warm-blooded woman would when thrown together in a physical situation with a virile and wildly attractive man. Even now her flesh burned like a torch, remembering how it had felt to lie naked in his arms, and that deep, raw longing that had awakened in her then clawed again like a hunger inside her.

What a fool she had been to believe that it was Paris that had bewitched her. The spell she'd been under had not been the spell of a city—but something far more dangerous. The spell of a man.

The realisation had knocked her sideways, for at once she had seen the mortal danger she was in. If she were to become emotionally involved with Matthew, what would become of her when the six months were up? A brief liaison would have its pleasures—at least, she had no doubt about that! But, equally, she knew for certain that it was not in her psyche to cope with casual affairs. Wasn't her emotional vulnerability the very reason for the armour she'd built up over the years? What madness had possessed her to shed it, even briefly, with a man as calculating and uncaring as Matthew Jordan?

Hence her very deliberate failure to offer an apology for the awful, untrue accusations she had made. Matthew had not behaved like an animal. On the contrary, he had revealed himself to be a sensitive and thoughtful lover. And before that belated attack of panic, she had been as eager for the picking as a ripe and juicy plum. Which was why she must never allow herself to run such a risk again. Though she burned with shame at the things she had said, it was safer to live with his anger and her guilt. Any attempt at a reconciliation could prove utterly fatal to her in the end.

As soon as they had arrived back at St Albans, Olivia had insisted on moving into the spare room—though it had to be said that Matthew's resistance to the arrangement had been little more than token. He doubtless had no more desire than she for a repeat of that ugly, demeaning scene.

But, convenient as their current sleeping arrangements had proved to be, they were bound to look curious to the eyes of a visitor. Especially when that visitor was a bright and sharp-eyed boy of sixteen.

'We can take the sofa-bed into my room,' Matthew had suggested, grim-faced, when Olivia had tentatively raised the subject. 'No one but ourselves need ever know that we're not in fact sleeping in the same bed.'

Even sleeping in the same room sounded risky to Olivia, though she could think of no better solution herself. She nodded vaguely, avoiding his eyes.

But, as usual, Matthew read her mind. 'Don't worry,' he told her, his tone stiff with sarcasm, 'for the duration of our cohabitation, I shall endeavour to keep my animal instincts under control.'

He succeeded manfully. The first couple of nights of Richard's stay, Olivia lay wide-eyed and sleepless in the big double bed—which, like a gentleman, Matthew had surrendered to her—and listened to the gentle rhythms of his breathing as he slept peacefully on the sofa-bed. It seemed he had more will-power than she, she found herself thinking with wry resentment. For, no matter how hard she tried to blot him from her consciousness, her senses were all too tinglingly aware of the vibrant, half-naked male presence lying just a few short feet away from her.

Even when she finally slept, her dreams were heated and disturbed. When she woke up in the morning, half exhausted and bleary-eyed, the object of her distraction had already vanished, leaving the sofa-bed all neatly folded in one corner, almost as though he had never been there.

At least the days were easier.

In spite of Richard's earlier reservations, and somewhat to Olivia's surprise, Matthew and her younger brother seemed to hit it off right from the word go—even before Matthew enigmatically revealed that he was working on a plan that would restore Richard's lost inheritance to him.

Did that mean that honour had finally won? Olivia asked herself on a prayer. Had he decided against the annulment? Had the transfer of Garland's been taken off 'hold'? When she questioned him, however, Matthew was evasive. 'You'll know when you need to know,' was all he would tell her.

Before Richard's arrival Olivia had worried that the tension in the house, already high, might rise to unbearable proportions with the addition of her brother. Richard was, after all, another potentially hostile Garland, and adolescent boys could be tiresome at times. Add to that the indisputable fact that Matthew's nerves were running on an exceedingly short fuse these days and you had the kind of volatile situation that could explode at any minute in your face.

But, contrary to all her fears, Richard's arrival on the scene had had the effect of oil on troubled waters, bringing out in Matthew yet another new and unsuspected side. He had gone to considerable trouble to keep his young guest occupied and amused. Today's gliding lesson had just been the latest in a string of riding trips and games of chess and endless sets of tennis on the private tennis courts. And it was perfectly clear to any observer that he had enjoyed himself every bit as much as Richard. The harsh lines that had darkened the handsome features of late were noticeably softened, and the old spark of humour was rekindled in his eyes.

And, though she remained as cautious as ever about keeping herself at a safe distance from him, with Richard to act as a kind of buffer, Olivia was aware of a definite lessening of hostility between the two of them. Once or twice there was even a momentary flash of that relaxed, easy closeness they had shared sporadically in Paris.

But the real eye-opener had been Matthew's runaway success with Richard. Almost hourly Olivia had seen the undisguised respect and admiration growing in her brother's eyes. 'I take back everything I ever said about him and the Jordans, Sis,' he had confided at the end of his first day. 'He's great! I'm really going to enjoy having him as a brother-in-law.'

Olivia had smiled tightly and glanced away, aware of a new weight pressing on her now. For suddenly she realised that when it came to explaining the divorce to her brother—in just under five months' time—she was not going to have an easy task on her hands.

It was undoubtedly all these conflicting anxieties and emotions that brought on the nightmare on the night before Richard was due to leave.

As usual, she had lain awake for hours, her brain teeming with seemingly insoluble problems. Then at last she had drifted off, only to be seized by an overwhelming terror, like some demon entering her soul. Next thing she was sitting up in bed, her body soaked in a lather of sweat, panting, her fingers clutching at the bedclothes, dimly aware that she was crying out.

'Hey, what's up, love? Relax. You're safe.' Even as she still struggled to regain her bearings, a warm, reassuring arm was stealing round her shoulder, drawing her still-shivering body against a broad and comforting chest. A strong, gentle hand smoothed her sweat-tousled hair. 'You're all right, Olivia,' a soft voice was telling her. 'I'm here with you. It was only a dream.'

Gratefully she leaned against him, her frightened, trembling fingers clutching at the rock-hard solidity of his arms, seeking, and somehow finding, a sense of security against the threat that still seemed to hover in the darkness all around her. As the bedside-lamp was suddenly snapped on Olivia blinked but did not move, feeling the wild race of her heart gradually start to slow as the safe and comforting presence at her side continued to hold her and stroke away her fear.

'Do you want me to bring you a glass of water?' Matthew enquired softly against her hair.

'No!' She tightened her grip impulsively on his arm, not wanting him to move away and leave her prey to the faceless menace still lurking out there in the shadows.

He was wearing nothing but a flimsy pair of dark blue silk pyjama bottoms. But, oddly, Olivia was not aware of his near-nakedness, only of his calm and comforting strength. Childlike, she pressed her pale-cheeked face against the smooth-muscled, dark-tanned chest, his warmth and the clean male scent of him like a healing balm to her shattered nerves. As hard, gentle arms closed protectively around her, she closed her eyes and heard him say, 'Do you want to tell me what the dream was about? The best way to drive a nightmare from your mind is simply to talk about it, I find.'

Olivia stole a glance at him, meeting the pair of frank, caring eyes that looked down from above a dark-stubbled jaw. She frowned slightly—surely a man like Matthew Jordan had never had a nightmare in his life?—then she answered truthfully, 'I can't remember. All I know is someone was chasing me and I was trying to get away. Only, my legs wouldn't move. My feet felt as though they were stuck to the ground.'

'A typical anxiety dream.' He stroked her hair and smiled a wry smile. 'I trust the villain of the piece wasn't me, by any chance?'

'I don't think so.' At the comforting note of humour in his voice, she allowed herself a tremulous smile. 'I'm not even sure if it was a person. It was just something scary. I couldn't even see it.'

Matthew drew the silky sheet around her shoulder and softly continued to stroke her hair, the leisurely, caressing movement acting like a tranquilliser to her senses. 'You've been letting things get to you, bottling up your emotions. I've been watching you over the weeks and I've seen it building up . . .'

Olivia shot him another glance, her eyes betraying her surprise.

'What's the matter?' he questioned mildly. 'Did you perhaps believe I was blind?'

Not blind, but she had assumed that, like most people, he was selective in the things he chose to observe. And surely her tormented state of mind would be the last thing to merit his attention? She shook her head and glanced away as he added, changing the subject subtly, 'Are you sure you wouldn't like me to get you something? A hot drink to help you sleep, perhaps?'

'No, thanks.' She shook her head again.

'OK.' Matthew bent to drop a light kiss on her hair. 'Is it all right if I put out the light?'

Olivia nodded as he reached out to switch off the lamp, then stiffened as she felt him slide from the bed. Involuntarily she tightened her grip on his arm. 'But don't leave me, Matthew. Not just yet.'

He paused. 'I'll stay as long as you like—but I hope you don't object if I join you underneath the covers. It's just a little bit chilly out here.' Then, when she didn't object, he pulled the sheet back and slid alongside her, his dark head resting on the pillow next to hers, his body warm as he pressed against her, gathering her more fully into his arms.

With a low, blissful moan Olivia snuggled closer, her soft, pliant body moulding to his, her head cushioned against one muscular shoulder as she slipped an innocent arm round his waist.

'Goodnight,' she heard him whisper. 'Sleep now, my love.'

'Goodnight,' she murmured in response. Then, on an impulse, she stole a glance at the finely carved jaw with its wide, sensitive mouth, at the strong, straight nose and the high, proud brow, and the eyes, closed now, with their long, thick lashes lying across his cheekbones like fringes of black silk. And all at once she knew she couldn't keep her gnawing guilt to herself any more. She took a deep breath and at last confessed, 'I'm sorry about what happened that last night in Paris. I was wrong to say the things I said.'

For a moment Matthew said nothing, and she could sense more than see the response in his face. Then his hand moved softly against her hair and, slowly, the long-lashed dark eyes opened. He smiled. 'Thank you for that,' he said. Then his fingers slid down to tilt her chin and she closed her eyes, her heart beating fast, as he bent to press warm lips to hers.

It was a far too brief and fleeting kiss, over almost before it had begun. Yet its subtle magic seemed to linger as Matthew murmured again, 'Sleep now,' and she closed her eyes and drifted away, happy in the warm, safe haven of his arms.

By the time she awoke next morning, feeling fresh after the best sleep she'd had in weeks, Olivia was once more alone in the big, warm double bed.

With a twinge almost of disappointment to discover Matthew already gone, she sat up and stretched, then suddenly caught sight of the lavishly wrapped package on the end of the bed. She paused and blinked. It was the package that contained the lingerie he had bought in Paris—and which she had believed was destined for Celine.

One peep inside confirmed that she was right. The exotic black nightdress and matching négligé nestled expensively in a bed of soft tissue. A little uneasily she laid it aside. What was this gesture supposed to mean?

Matthew was on the point of leaving as she walked into the breakfast-room. Dressed in his customary weekday attire of dark suit, light shirt and bright silk tie, he quickly drained his coffee-cup and grinned up at her as she walked in. 'Hi there! Good morning. I trust you slept well?'

'Yes, thanks—extremely well,' Olivia acknowledged a trifle formally. All at once, just at the sight of him, a rush of warmth had spread through her veins and her heart was doing crazy gymnastics, cavorting around inside her chest. Abruptly she turned her eyes towards Richard, who was piling marmalade on to a roll. 'Hi there,' she greeted him cheerfully, still uncomfortably aware of Matthew's dark eyes on her face.

'Morning, Sis. You're looking well today,' he responded, causing the pink in her cheeks to deepen.

She sat down at the table opposite her brother, just as Matthew rose to his feet. 'I'd better be off,' she heard him say as she studiously poured orange juice into a glass. Then he was bending to plant a distinctly warmer and less hurried than usual farewell kiss on her lips. 'I'll see you this evening,' he murmured against her ear. Then he straightened and reached out to tousle Richard's hair. 'Have a good journey back,' he told him with a smile. 'And be sure to come and visit us again just as soon as you can.'

'Don't worry, I will.' Richard rose to his feet and held out his hand, a gleam of affection and respect in his wide, bright, youthful eyes. 'And thanks for everything,' he added sincerely. 'It's been a really terrific weekend.'

'I'm pleased to hear you enjoyed yourself.' Matthew smiled back at the boy as he warmly accepted the proffered hand. 'I enjoyed it too. In fact, I think it did all of us quite a lot of good.' Dark hazel eyes sought Olivia's for a moment, then he winked at her. 'I'll be back early tonight.'

Richard left on the one o'clock train, and it was a deeply disturbed Olivia who drove back alone from the railway station.

Last night, she realised belatedly, had been a terrible and ghastly mistake. The hostility between herself and Matthew that she relied upon to protect herself had already been dangerously eroded since the arrival of Richard. Last night it had dissolved altogether, leaving her mortally exposed. She had even, insanely, apologised and spent the night wrapped in his arms! And now—with that kiss, that wink, the lingerie—it looked alarmingly as though he expected this state of *détente* to continue.

But it mustn't! She shivered at the thought. To

allow herself to get any closer to him would be nothing less than suicide on her part. Though she dreaded the thought of a confrontation, somehow —and quickly, before this misunderstanding had time to develop—she must make it very clear to him that last night had been no more than an aberration.

Olivia kept herself busy that afternoon, making various phone calls to Chester to keep in touch with old colleagues and allies. From The Gallery, Jeffrey Parker assured her that both the business and Sydney, the cat, were thriving quite happily in her absence. But to her surprise, when she tried to contact Lewis at his office, she was told by his new deputy, Arthur McKay, that he had gone off on holiday.

'He went off last Friday,' he further enlightened her when she enquired. Then, 'Sorry, I'm afraid he didn't say where he was going.'

How very curious, Olivia found herself thinking as she laid down the phone. Though he was perfectly entitled, of course, to go off when and where he pleased, it wasn't like Lewis to disappear like this without letting her know. Still, it wasn't really so surprising in the present circumstances, she decided. The poor man had probably been desperate for a break. These days it couldn't be very pleasant for him working in the shadow of Arthur McKay.

Mercifully, things would be getting back to normal fairly soon. In just five months, with Garland's back in Garland hands, Lewis would finally have McKay off his back and would be able to get back to running the company as efficiently as he always had.

In the meantime . . . Olivia glanced at her watch . . . she had much more pressing matters on her mind. Matthew had threatened to come home early, and it was already four o'clock!

It was just fifteen minutes later that she heard the Rolls come up the drive. Nervously she rose to her feet, adjusting the cuffs of her long-sleeved blouse and smoothing her tightly chignoned hair as she inwardly rehearsed for the hundredth time the carefully reasoned little speech she had prepared that would set things straight between them once and for all.

She would be neither disagreeable nor aggressive, just firm and logical and composed. She would explain to him in calm and rational terms that she was psychologically incapable of coping with the sort of short-term physical relationship that he, quite clearly, still had in mind. She would leave aside the feelings he aroused in her—the excitement, the fear, the overpowering need. She still barely understood them herself, and their intrusion would only serve to complicate things. Instead she would simply appeal to his finer side, a side she had growing reason to believe did exist, and pray that he would have enough respect for her to agree to her not unreasonable demands.

He walked through the sitting-room doorway and instantly took her breath away. 'Hello there! Had a good day?' In a couple of strides he had crossed to where she was standing and deposited a warm, lingering kiss on her lips.

Dry-mouthed, Olivia backed away. 'Not bad,'

she answered numbly, avoiding his gaze. Suddenly her little welcoming speech had evaporated clean out of her head.

Matthew seemed blissfully unaware of her sudden state of consternation. With long, strong fingers, he loosened his tie. 'I think I'll just nip upstairs and have a quick shower and change.' He paused to drop another burning kiss on her mouth. 'How about preparing us a drink while I'm gone?'

'Fine,' she agreed with a brief, brisk nod. Then she paused to watch him as he headed for the door, half hypnotised in spite of herself by the broad, strong shoulders, the smooth, supple back. What a pity that such a splendid creature should pose such a cruel threat to her!

But he did, and she must deal with it. And, what was more, she must deal with it right now. Mentally, she gave herself a shake. While he was gone, she must re-gather her wits and and be ready the minute he walked back through the door to launch relentlessly into her argument. She crossed to the drinks cabinet and poured herself a stiff Martini and Matthew's habitual Scotch. Over a civilised drink would be the perfect setting for her to state her case.

Alas, she never got the chance. She had just seated herself on the red velvet sofa when suddenly the door burst open and Matthew came charging into the room like a raging bull. He was still wearing the business suit he'd arrived in, though his good humour had vanished beneath an ebony scowl.

He came marching up to the sofa and stood over her threateningly. 'I'd like an explanation—right now!' he thundered.

Instinctively, Olivia backed against the cushions. 'An explanation of what?' she demanded, forcing herself to meet his eyes. Then, though she suspected that really she knew very well, she shot at him defiantly, 'I don't know what you're talking about!'

'You know damned well what I'm talking about!' His tone was like meat-hooks impaling live flesh, his expression murderous as he went on, 'You've moved your things back into the spare room. Perhaps you'd be good enough to explain why?'

So it was exactly as she'd thought. Nothing escaped those laser-beam eyes. But though this afternoon, when she had made the move, she'd anticipated his displeasure, it had never crossed her mind that she would have to face anger on this terrible scale. She looked back at him as steadily as she could. 'My moving into your room was merely a temporary arrangement, for the sake of appearances while Richard was here. Surely you knew I'd move out again as soon as he'd gone?'

Dark hazel eyes flashed unforgivingly. 'Not after last night, I didn't!' he snapped.

'Last night?' Olivia narrowed her eyes, assuming an air of incomprehension. 'I wasn't aware of anything of particular significance happening last night.'

'Oh, no?' He was standing right over her, his face a dark, satanic mask of fury. 'In that case, perhaps I was the one who was having dreams, not you,' he ground sarcastically. 'But I distinctly remember that we spent the entire night wrapped in each other's arms.'

The memory brought a flush to her cheeks. For a moment she could feel again the delicious warmth of his flesh against hers, the sweet softness of his breath in her hair and the safe, hard, sensuous strength of those powerful arms locking their bodies together. 'That didn't mean a thing!' she protested. 'You know very well why we spent the night together—because I was scared, that was all!'

'To begin with, I'll grant you. But it wasn't just out of fear that you invited me to stay.' Contemptuously he held her eyes. 'I got the distinct impression that you quite enjoyed sharing a bed with me.'

The barb was rather close to the truth for comfort. Olivia's fists clenched in self-defence. 'Did you?' she flung at him, determined to meet scorn with scorn. 'Well, not quite enough, I'm afraid, to want to make a habit of it! So sorry to disappoint you, but I'm afraid your fatal charm didn't quite work last night!'

She should not have said that. Matthew was in no mood for flippant gibes. Before she knew what was happening, he had reached out and grabbed her by the arm, lifting her bodily from the sofa, spinning her round roughly so that her body was jammed against his. 'Don't play games!' he ground at her. 'I've already had more than enough of your games! Over the past few weeks, since we got back from Paris, I've been more than patient with you. I didn't say a thing when you kept hiding yourself away in that damned spare room every time I walked through the door. But don't expect my patience to endure much longer. You're my wife, remember. It's time you realised the full implications of that and started behaving accordingly!'

'Or what?' she demanded. 'Are you threatening me again?'

Matthew did not answer, just looked at her with granite hazel eyes as, angrily, she struggled to free herself from his grip on her arm.

'Why won't you get it into your head that you're wasting your time?' she seethed. 'Just because we made a deal that involved marriage, am I supposed to make my body available to you? Am I supposed to behave like some kind of whore?'

Again she struggled futilely as he continued to hold her firm, her blue eyes flashing with sudden venom as she railed against him in helpless fury. 'I told you at the start that there's only one way you'll ever make me give in, and that's by using brute force—which I'm sure you've got plenty of! But I can think of nothing more repugnant than being made love to by a man like you!' Her lips curled to illustrate her distaste. 'You're a cheap opportunist and a bully. The very thought of any form of physical contact with you at all literally makes me sick!'

It was way, way over the top, and she knew it, besides being a million miles from the truth. Once, maybe, some of it might have applied, but alas, no longer. Which was precisely why she glared up at him with cold and unrepentant eyes as he continued to hold her in his grip. Somehow she had to protect herself from the powerful and potentially fatal attraction that Matthew wielded over her. And if she had to go to extremes to do it, then the end justified the means.

White-lipped, his face rigid with anger, Matthew stared at her in silence for a moment, and there was a dark and fearsome glint in his eyes, like a dangerous animal provoked too far. Olivia steeled herself for the onslaught as she felt his grip tighten around her arm, but when he eventually spoke his voice was low and carefully controlled. 'In that case, I shall relieve you of my presence.' Roughly he flung her back down on the sofa and, abruptly, turned away. 'Sleep in any bed you like tonight! Sleep in hell for all I care! I won't be here to bother you—I'm going to spend the night in London!'

For a long time after the door had slammed behind him and she had heard the Rolls growl off down the drive, Olivia remained crouched on the sofa, her head in her hands, feeling faintly sick and shaky. Once again she had ended up behaving in a manner of which she felt deeply ashamed. In spite of the threat he posed her, Matthew had not deserved that torrent of abuse. What was it about the man that drove her to such vindictive excesses?

All evening she could not shake off her guilt. She ate hardly at all, picking without appetite at a piece of poached fish. Then she poured herself a drink and sat on the sofa, her eyes drifting constantly towards the phone. Perhaps she should call him and say she was sorry? She felt sure he would be at the flat at Regent's Park. But a phone call could sound so impersonal, and what if he hung up on her? She knew she wouldn't sleep a wink tonight until she had set things straight.

Resolutely she got to her feet. That meant there was only one thing to do. She would drive down to London herself and offer her apology personally.

She changed quickly, into one of the outfits they had bought in Paris—a soft blue dress with a wide leather belt that Matthew particularly liked. Then she unpinned her hair and brushed it to her shoulders in a deliberately conciliatory gesture. However angry he might still be, he would surely realise the instant he saw her that she had come on a mission of peace.

She took the Mercedes that he had put at her disposal and headed south, driving as fast as the traffic would allow—all the while rehearsing, yet again, the little speech she had prepared that afternoon. This time there must be no hiccups. She had to get it right first time. For suddenly it was vitally important to her that she and Matthew find a way to live out the next few months together in some kind of harmony.

She did not want him to be her enemy, to see again that look of cold contempt in his eyes. Though she would never dare let him become her lover, surely they could be friends?

At last, with beating heart, she drew up outside the elegant Nash terrace and squinted up at the second-floor windows. She had been right; he was here. In spite of the late hour, the lights were burning brightly.

Too nervous to wait for the elevator, she sprinted up the stairs, anxiety quickening in her breast as she reached the front door and pressed the bell. It seemed like an interminably long time until she heard the latch being drawn back, then her stomach squeezed with illogical pleasure as the door finally opened and Matthew was standing there.

He was dressed as he had been when he had stormed out of the house, only he had shed his jacket and tie. But the buttons of the crisp white shirt were undone to half-way down his chest, the sleeves rolled back to the elbows, giving him a faintly dishevelled look. Even the sleek dark hair looked rumpled, and he wore the impatient frown of a man who had just been most inconveniently disturbed. He took one look at Olivia and growled, 'What the hell are you doing here?'

Olivia smiled apologetically. Perhaps he had been on his way to bed. 'Matthew, can we talk?' she began. 'I know it's late, but I had to——'

But that was as far as she got. Before she could even finish her sentence, she was interrupted by a purring female voice. 'Matthew darling . . . who is it?'

And Olivia felt the blood drain from her face and a cold Baltic chill creep through her bones as a tousled blonde figure in a thin silk robe appeared in a doorway at the end of the hall.

Of course. She should have guessed why Matthew appeared so grumpy and so dishevelled. She had just had the gross effrontery to disturb him while he was busy entertaining the delectable Celine.

CHAPTER EIGHT

THE CHILLING events of the hour that followed were branded forever on Olivia's brain.

Her first instinct was to turn and run, to retreat with her hurt and humiliation and hide herself away. For, unlikely and out of place as they might be, those were the emotions that ripped through her soul at the sight of the blonde figure in the ruby silk robe standing brazenly watching her from the end of the hallway. And more than just hurt and humiliation—a mindless, illogical, ravening wrench of naked, primitive jealousy.

But even as she stood poised for flight in the doorway, bitter bile rising in her throat, her innate reserves of dignity and strength chose this timely moment to come to her aid. Very deliberately she straightened and levelled cold blue eyes at the blonde Celine. 'What do you think you're doing here with my husband?' she demanded imperiously. 'Kindly put on some clothes and get out of our house immediately!'

Celine was visibly taken aback by the response. It was as though she had been expecting Olivia to slink off with her tail between her legs. The heavily mascaraed eyes flicked across to Matthew, awaiting his command, and Olivia fancied she detected the merest hint of dark amusement through the more evident anger etched across his features as, with a silent but expressive gesture, he indicated to his secretary to go.

Then, as the blonde girl reluctantly retreated into the bedroom from which she had emerged, he stood aside with derisive deference to allow Olivia into the hall. 'So, to what do I owe this hysterical intrusion?' he enquired in a cutting tone.

As Olivia followed him into the sitting-room, her stomach was a nest of squirming vipers. She didn't bother to answer his snide enquiry. Instead, mildly surprised at the outrage in her voice, she instantly shot back one of her own. 'What's that female doing here? I thought you told me you didn't believe in adultery?'

As he turned to confront her, hands thrust arrogantly into the pockets of his trousers, more than a hint of a cruel, mocking smile glittered in the dark hazel eyes. He held her gaze. 'And I thought you told me you did?' he countered. 'You were the one who made a point of spelling out, so romantically, on our wedding night, that I was free to indulge in whatever extra-marital activities I wished.' The dark eyes narrowed questioningly as, slowly, he looked her up and down. 'Why this sudden change of heart?'

Why, indeed? Olivia was wondering to herself. She ought to be delighted by this turn of events—or indifferent, at the very least. This attack of vicious, gnawing resentment made no sense at all. Struggling to get a grip on her renegade emotions, she managed to sound almost convincing as she assured him now in a clipped, tight voice, 'Don't worry, I haven't had a change of heart. It's just that I'd hoped you might have the taste to be a little more discreet about your affairs.'

He raised one logical dark eyebrow at her, dismissing the patently irrational claim. 'And what could be more discreet than this? You're the one who's lacking in taste, coming here spying in the middle of the night!'

'Spying? Is that why you think I'm here?'

'And why else would you have come here?' Matthew challenged her.

It was her cue to break into her long-prepared and carefully rehearsed speech, but the now fully clad Celine chose that moment to re-emerge from the bedroom and come clicking down the hallway on impudently high heels. At the front door she turned and paused to cast a leisurely glance over her shoulder in the direction of the sitting-room. Then, once she was certain that she had Olivia's attention, she raised one blood-red manicured hand and fluttered a fond farewell towards Matthew. 'See you later,' she mouthed. Then, with a geisha-like swing of her shapely hips, she made a graceful and unhurried exit.

The defiant spectacle had the instantaneous effect of driving all Olivia's good intentions from her head. Why should she bother to put her case to him in some pointless effort to bring harmony into their lives? The parlous state of their relationship was evidently the last thing on *his* mind!

He was still waiting for an answer to his question as to why she had so unexpectedly turned up on the scene. She hastened to assure him, 'Don't worry. To spy on you is not why I'm here. As I've already made quite clear to you, I don't give a damn what you get up to. Though I must say,' she added with a deliberate twist of distaste, 'I find the total lack of discrimination with which you pursue your carnal appetites just a little bit unsettling. Only a matter of hours ago you were planning to lure *me* into your bed. Now I find you virtually in the process of slaking your lust with your secretary. Bed-hopping is evidently a pursuit at which you excel. Alleycats, I believe, share a similar set of moral standards.'

As she finished her malicious diatribe, the hazel eyes narrowed dangerously and the muscles of the powerful shoulders seemed to bunch threateningly beneath the thin white shirt. His tone, as he answered her, was sharded glass, each syllable designed to wound and tear apart. 'Perhaps, in your book, a man is an alleycat because he has normal sexual desires. But with due respect, I would suggest that normal sexual desires are not something you know much about.' Eyes like bayonets drove through her. 'If anyone around here has a sexual problem, that one is you, my dear Olivia, not I.'

Inwardly Olivia winced, but she willed herself to hide how much his words had hurt. 'What a typically arrogant male response! Just because I don't fancy having sex with you, I'm supposed to have some kind of sexual problem!'

Bitter amusement curled at Matthew's lip. 'The arrogance is yours, not mine. Do you seriously expect me to believe what you've just said?

Perhaps you've forgotten what happened—or *almost* happened—on our last night in Paris? There was no mistaking the fact that you fancied having sex with me then.' He let his eyes slide over her, their expression crudely provocative. 'Believe me, I know when a woman is aroused, and you were highly aroused that night.'

Damn him, did he have no shame? Olivia burned from her hair down to her toes at the unchivalrous, though manifestly true, observation. 'I'd been drinking!' she denied. 'It was the drink that made me react the way I did. It had nothing to do with you!'

'Oh, no?' He smiled a piranha smile. 'And have you been drinking now?'

She glared at him. 'No. Why do you ask?'

Again that smile that sent goose-bumps down her spine. 'I was thinking that perhaps we might conduct a control experiment, just to see if there's any truth in your denials.' With a panther's stride he took a step towards her, almost before she could read what he had in mind. 'Come here, my little wife,' he purred, reaching out to catch hold of her arm. His gaze glided over her soft, loose hair, the subtle, clinging lines of the chic blue dress. 'Besides, I have more than the faintest suspicion that this is what you really came for.'

'Oh, no, you don't!' Just a fraction too late, Olivia recoiled. He was too strong and much too quick for her. Already her body was clamped against his, held firm by the iron-hard fist at her waist. As her breasts were pressed against the hard wall of his chest and the heat of his muscular thighs devoured her, she dug her fingers into the flesh of his shoulders and struggled violently to tear herself free.

With ease he caught one of her hands in his and jerked it unceremoniously behind her back. 'So you're going to make it difficult, are you?' He smiled at her with devilish enjoyment. 'That's OK, I quite enjoy a fight.'

'You bastard! Let me go!' She was squirming as helplessly as a sprat caught in a polar bear's paw, tears of frustration brimming in her eyes as she continued to beat against his shoulder with her one remaining fist. 'Get your hands off me this minute! I demand that you let me go!'

'Demand?' He seemed to find the notion amusing. 'Would you deny your husband a kiss?'

'You're not my husband! Let me go! You're not my husband—you have no right!'

'Oh, no?' One dark eyebrow arched at her as her remaining free hand was grabbed in turn and pinned securely behind her back. 'I think I have a piece of paper somewhere that would indicate that I am indeed your lawful husband. And husbands, my dear Olivia, happen to have certain rights!'

Olivia's heart gave a nervous lurch as he proceeded to immobilise her totally now, his grip on her two pinioned wrists tightening slightly as the fingers of his free hand jabbed roughly through her loose, dark hair, dragging her head backwards, so that she gasped, her lips parting involuntarily as his mouth came down to conquer hers.

It was a fierce, almost brutal kiss, designed to

crush all resistance from her. Yet, beyond its iron domination that all her instincts rose up against, there was a raw, underlying sensuality, a masculine, thrusting, bone-melting passion that the woman in her could not but respond to. Fire licked through her senses, sending sheets of hot longing sweeping through her veins.

She gasped as Matthew began to deepen his kiss and the hand in her hair moved deliciously downwards to capture the warm, eager weight of her breasts. Cruel fingers mercilessly teased the tightly burgeoning, aching peaks, sending a jolt of white-hot desire piercing wantonly through her loins.

Where was her denial that he could arouse her now? Washed away like flotsam on the tide of longing that his touch and his kiss had unleashed in her. Her hungry body was limp and quivering as his wild, carnal onslaught on her senses continued. And, in spite of herself, the hands still held captive behind her back longed secretly to be released, so that they might freely twine themselves around the strong male shoulders and let her fingers loose in the thick, dark hair.

A helpless prisoner in his arms, she ached with every sinew for liberation so that, at last, she might give expression to the fire that raged within her soul.

And yet when, abruptly, Matthew let her go, she found herself responding physically in total contradiction to the emotional dictates of her heart. As the brooding dark eyes burned down at her, scouring the secrets of her soul, she took a step back and, with all her strength, landed him a blow across the side of his face. Her hand was stinging as she dropped it to her side, mingled shock and satisfaction flooding through her at the sight of the red welt across his jaw. 'How dare you, you bastard!' she spat, still struggling to control her trembling limbs. 'I don't know what you supposed you proved with that.'

Matthew smiled thinly. 'I think you're the one who's just supplied the proof.' Tentatively, he touched his jaw. 'You wanted me all right back there, but those damned sexual hang-ups of yours won in the end.'

With a contemptuous gesture he turned away, unmoved by the distraught look in her eyes. For, suddenly, Olivia would have given anything in the world to be able to undo that hasty slap. With an oddly bereft sensation she watched as he crossed to the sofa where his jacket and tie were draped, longing to apologise, but too proud, as he pulled on the jacket and stuffed the tie into his pocket.

'Spend the night here if you want to,' he was saying. 'It's a little late to think of driving back. And don't worry,' he added without emotion, 'I won't be here to bother you.'

'Where are you going?' Wishing she could think of some way to stop him, she watched as he headed for the door. Then, her tone betraying the bitterness she felt, she added accusingly, 'You're going after Celine, aren't you?'

Matthew paused in the doorway and fixed her with an unforgiving eye. 'I'm going where the hell I please,' he informed her. 'And it's really none of your damned business.' He strode across the hall without a backward glance, then paused to deliver his parting shot.

'As I said, you can spend the night here . . . but kindly do me the infinite favour of being gone by tomorrow morning. And the even more infinite favour,' he added for good measure, 'of keeping your distance from me from now on!'

After that, things went from bad to worse.

Matthew was spending virtually no time at all at the house at St Albans. He was sleeping there during the week, presumably because of the convenient proximity of the house to his office, but he took none of his meals at home and Olivia was usually already in bed long before he showed up in the evenings.

The weekends he spent in London—at the Regent's Park flat with Celine, she guessed. For he made no secret of the fact that he was seeing the girl again. And, even if he had chosen to keep it quiet, Olivia had almost certain proof. On at least a dozen occasions over the last couple of weeks, Celine had phoned to the house, requesting as bold as brass, 'I'd like to speak to Matthew, please.'

No more 'Mr Jordan', Olivia thought with a strange, dull ache. Suddenly no one was even pretending to be civil any more.

On the very rare occasions when Matthew's and Olivia's paths had crossed, they had barely acknowledged one another. 'Celine called,' she told him, hating the way it hurt her just to pronounce the name, feeling even more chilled by his uncaring answer.

'I know. I've spoken to her since.'

Yet why should he act otherwise? she tried to tell herself. She was the one who was reacting illogically to the situation. No bonds, no commitment—that had been the deal from the very start. This marriage of theirs was nothing but a front. It was never intended to be more.

And they were still married—no more talk of annulment—so there was still a good chance that she would get Garland's back. Plus she had the additional bonus that Matthew was hardly ever there.

So why, when she should be feeling hopeful, was she so unutterably miserable? Why did she resent his absences? Why did his uncaring comments hurt? And above all, why was she virtually eaten alive by jealousy every time Celine's name cropped up?

With an effort, she swept such questions from her head, knowing in her soul what the answer must be, yet knowing also that she was too afraid to face its brutal implications.

It was a couple of weeks after the episode with Celine at the Regent's Park flat that Olivia found herself involved in another, equally tacky, confrontation.

It was early afternoon on the housekeeper's day off, and Olivia had taken a sun-lounger out on to the front terrace to enjoy a bit of early June sun. Hearing the phone ring, she laid down her magazine and hurried inside to the drawing-room to answer it.

It was Matthew, and he came straight to the point. 'I left in something of a hurry this morning,' he told her, 'and I seem to have left a file of papers behind.' His tone was businesslike but polite as he requested, 'Do you think you could do me a favour, please, and just check that it's there? It should be on the bureau beside my bed.'

'Of course. Hang on while I check.' Just the sound of his voice had set her pulses fluttering, and as she laid down the phone and hurried upstairs she was aware of an excited tightening in her chest. That brief but, for once, quite civil exchange had warmed the cold, empty quarters of her heart, and there was something quite illogically pleasing in the way he had requested this small favour of her.

A moment later, with a squeeze of emotion, she pushed open his bedroom door. It was the first time she had been inside it since the day that Richard had left. And suddenly the memory of that sweet night together went flooding through her, pinkening her cheeks. Silly, she chided herself, as she darted past the bed to the bureau, noting with satisfaction the big blue file that was sitting there.

She picked up the phone extension by the bed. 'It's here,' she told Matthew, keeping her tone cool. 'What would you like me to do with it?'

'Just hang on to it, if you don't mind. I'll be over to collect it in about half an hour.'

With the file clasped safely to her bosom, Olivia made her way downstairs again, aware of an unmistakable lift in her spirits at the thought of seeing him. In the hall, she paused briefly before the big bronze mirror to fluff her fingers through her loose, shiny hair, glad that she was wearing one of her more flattering white tops and a particularly pretty, flouncy summer skirt.

The prim image Matthew had once accused her of was something she had almost unconsciously discarded over the weeks since their return from Paris. Not that Matthew had ever commented. He was rarely around to see her, for a start. But, even without his seal of approval, she found her new, more stylish, yet more relaxed way of dressing lent her a new inward poise and pleasure in herself.

Little did she know that, in just a moment, her precious poise was about to be shattered.

She was back on the terrace, trying to look casual, sitting on the sun-bed flicking unseeingly through the pages of her magazine, when the Rolls appeared at the end of the drive. With a flash of nerves she straightened and touched her hair, allowing a light smile to hover around her lips. Welcoming, but cautiously so.

A moment later her smile fell apart and every muscle in her body went painfully rigid. For, as the big midnight blue car came sweeping towards her, she could see all too clearly that it was not Matthew at the wheel. With an effort she gritted her teeth, fighting back a wave of helpless hurt and anger, as the car door swung open and Celine stepped coquettishly out on to the drive.

She was wearing a skimpy, bright green tube dress that moulded the shapely contours of her generous bosom and softly curved thighs, the

blonde hair carefully teased into a mane that
framed her cleverly made-up face. In bitter
dejection, Olivia watched as she sashayed the
short distance to the terrace. Small wonder
Matthew was forgetfully leaving things behind
when he had such a voluptuous creature on his
mind!

A smug smile curved the shiny red lips as, on
perilously spindly heels, the blonde girl
approached the immobile figure sitting stiff and
straight-backed on the sun-lounger. 'I'm afraid
Matthew got caught up in a meeting,' she cooed,
the geisha eyes scanning Olivia's taut, drawn face,
totally devoid of colour now. She fluttered darkly
mascaraed lashes. 'So he sent me over to pick up
the file.'

With fingers whose trembling she could barely
control, Olivia reached for the file on the little table
at her side and, without rising, handed it to her.
'This is it, I think,' she said.

The shiny lips parted to reveal perfect pearly
teeth. 'Is it all there?' Celine wanted to know.

Olivia hesitated. 'I don't know.' She didn't even
know what the file contained.

Another pearly smile. 'I'd better check.' Then,
clearly relishing every minute of this humiliating
scenario, Celine proceeded to lower her curvy hips
on to the edge of the sun-lounger next to Olivia,
clearly feeling as much at home here as she
evidently did in the Regent's Park flat. Elaborately,
she crossed pale-stockinged legs, the hem of her
dress riding up to mid-thigh as she unhurriedly
opened up the file and in leisurely fashion

examined its contents.

Olivia had a sudden flash of her sitting alluringly in Matthew's office, taking instructions for the day, and was seized by an almost overpowering desire to snatch the file from her hands and fling it in her face. Somehow she restrained herself, forcing herself to breathe calmly and deeply, even managing the faded semblance of a smile as, slowly, Celine uncrossed her legs and began to get to her feet again.

'It appears to be all here,' she confirmed, tossing another pearly smile at Olivia as she smoothed the green dress down over her hips. 'I'll go now and leave you to get on with your sunbathing. Matthew's in a dreadful hurry for this stuff.'

'Don't worry, I wouldn't want to keep you,' Olivia assured her with deadly sincerity as she headed off towards the car.

But Celine had the similingly poisonous last word. As she reached the Rolls, she paused and turned, the geisha eyes fixed triumphantly on Olivia's pale face. 'Oh, by the way . . . Matthew and I will be away for a couple of days. Brussels. Strictly business, of course.' She pulled the car door open and added as she slid inside, 'I'm sure he's already told you, of course, but I thought I'd better mention it, just in case it had slipped his mind.'

Next minute the Rolls was whispering silently down the drive, while, dry-mouthed, Olivia watched it go. Of course she had known nothing of the 'strictly business' trip to Brussels, as Celine had undoubtedly been fully aware.

Stiffly she clambered to her feet and staggered indoors, feeling sick and sore inside. Surely this must be my ultimate humiliation, she was thinking. But, sadly, she was wrong.

'I reckon it's time the two of us sat down and had a little talk.'

For the first time in nearly a month Matthew had come home for dinner. He had phoned from the office to let Olivia know, and she had spent a nervously excited afternoon in the kitchen preparing something special for their meal. She had no idea what was behind the move, but she was hopeful it might have something positive to do with them. Perhaps even at this late stage, she was praying, some more amicable arrangement could be worked out between them.

Her fond hopes had withered slightly the moment he'd walked through the door. The grim, unsmiling expression on his face was not that of a man bent on reconciliation. But throughout the meal—that he had barely touched and Olivia had barely tasted—he had failed to reveal what was on his mind. Only now, as she poured coffee in the drawing-room and nervously handed him his cup, did he finally come out with what their little talk was to be about.

'I've finally managed to unravel the mystery of my uncle Roland's deal with your mother.'

She met the dark eyes with a stab of disappointment. So it was not their own relationship that was to be the subject of their discussion. 'Oh?' was all she could think of to say as she waited for him to elaborate.

He did not continue immediately, but stared for a long and thoughtful moment into the fine porcelain coffee-cup. As Olivia watched him, she could not help but notice the lines of tiredness and the pools of dark shadow that seemed to tug at his mouth and eyes. Too many late nights with Celine, she thought bitterly to herself, as at last he glanced up at her and, seeming to change the subject, asked, 'Have you heard from Ottley recently?'

Olivia frowned. 'Lewis? No. I tried to phone him a couple of weeks ago, but I was told he'd gone off on holiday.'

An ironic smile played round the wide, carved lips. 'Holiday?' Matthew repeated, apparently amused. 'Something of an extended holiday, I suspect.' Shrewd hazel eyes looked into hers. 'Don't expect to see your Mr Ottley back.'

What a peculiar thing to suggest! 'Why ever not?' Olivia asked.

The frown between the dark brows deepened as Matthew stared into his coffee-cup again. 'To put it crudely,' he told her, 'your dear Lewis Ottley has done a bunk.'

Now he was talking in riddles. 'And why on earth should he do that?'

Matthew sighed. 'I realise that what I'm about to tell you may be a little hard for you to take in, but I assure you I wouldn't be saying it if I didn't have incontrovertible proof. The reason you won't be seeing Ottley again is that he's finally been found out. He's been fleecing Garland's for years, but it took McKay to finally pin him down.'

Olivia was listening, open-mouthed. 'I don't know what you're talking about,' she told him, patently disbelieving. 'And what has any of this got to do with your uncle Roland and my mother?'

'I'll explain.' He leaned back in his chair, drained his coffee-cup and laid it to one side. 'The story goes back a very long way—to immediately after your father died. There's no evidence that Ottley was stealing while your father was alive, but when your mother put him in charge of operations, he apparently found the temptation too much. And he's a clever man. An accountant who knows his stuff.' He paused to hold her eyes for a moment before going on, 'He might have got away with it forever if your mother hadn't married Uncle Roland. Unfortunately for Mr Ottley, Uncle Roland was just as clever.'

He took a deep breath and ran long, tanned fingers across his thick, dark hair. 'Uncle Roland apparently suspected that something not quite right was going on—for the simple reason that it seemed to him that, considering its turnover, Garland's wasn't making quite the profits it should have been making. He made preliminary investigations, but came up against a brick wall. As I told you, your Mr Ottley is a very clever crook. So—and this is the bit that will interest you most—with your mother's approval, Uncle Roland arranged to take Garland's under Jordan's wing for a while, partly to see if he could uncover what was going on and partly to help your mother's company recoup some of the losses it was unaccountably making.

'However,' he smiled and raised one dark eyebrow at her as he elaborated with evident pleasure, 'written into the agreement that your mother and my uncle made was a special clause designed specifically to protect Garland's from old Uncle Julius's inheritance clause—the one that prohibits any part of Jordan's passing into non-family hands. This special clause set out quite clearly that Richard had the right to have the company returned to him at the age of twenty-one—or to remain as part of Jordan's and opt for a deal not dissimilar to the one I was proposing,' he added pointedly.

Olivia was poised on the edge of her seat. It was like listening to a fairy story. 'So how come we didn't know all this before?' she put to him, still openly sceptical.

Matthew nodded. 'I'm coming to that.' Then he leaned towards her as he carried on, 'The merger was kept a secret to avoid raising Ottley's suspicions—for, like me, Uncle Roland suspected Ottley from the start. And, as it happens, his tactics paid off. Back in January he finally laid hands on conclusive proof of how Ottley was cooking the books. He was getting ready to make criminal charges when, tragically, he and your mother were killed in that skiing accident.'

As Olivia's gaze flickered and she lowered her eyes, Matthew went on in a more sympathetic tone, 'By this time Ottley had wind of what was up, so this was when he made his truly inspired move. He broke into the Jordan computer and erased all evidence of the charges against him, along with all the details of the merger. He was greedy, you see, and that was his downfall. If he'd allowed the details of the merger to remain on record, he would have had to wait till Richard was twenty-one before he could get control of Garland's again—and even then he couldn't be sure that Richard might not opt to remain as part of Jordan's.'

A wry smile curled around his lips. 'That's why, he was so keen to back you up in your bid to get Garland's back, even to the extent of encouraging you to marry me.' He sighed and leaned back heavily in his chair again. 'McKay managed to find all this out through a recently retired secretary who used to work for my uncle Roland. Not being of a generation totally dedicated to computers, she'd kept some paper files on my uncle's findings regarding Ottley and the merger as well. On a hunch, McKay dug her out of retirement, and suddenly all the evidence fell into our hands . . .'

He paused in his monologue and shook his head. 'Unfortunately, Ottley's spies must have been looking out for him, for, as you discovered for yourself, he conveniently disappeared off on holiday just a couple of weeks ago. My guess is we've seen the last of him. He's probably taken off for Brazil or somewhere to live out the rest of his life in comfort on his ill-gotten gains.'

Olivia felt as though her brain had turned to papier mâché. How could any of this be true of a man she had trusted so implicitly? Still suspicious, she squinted at Matthew. 'Why did you say that you suspected him right from the start?'

Matthew shrugged. 'It was instinct, largely. I had an instant feeling about the man.' Then a half-serious smile tugged at his lips. 'Besides, my mother always warned me never to trust a man who wears a ring on his middle finger.'

So he was making a joke out of it! Somehow that was typical! But before she could come back at him, he continued, resuming his former sober tone, 'Now that we know the details of the agreement between my uncle and your mother, the choice of what happens next is entirely up to you. We can go ahead with our current plan to hand Garland's back to you in a few months' time . . .' He paused and deliberately held her eyes. 'I had the official transfer documents drafted shortly after our return from Paris. All they're waiting for now is a signature.'

So the annulment threat had been just that, a threat. Matthew had never really intended reneging on their deal. As Olivia dropped her eyes, peculiarly relieved, he carried on with what he'd been saying.

'Or, if you like, we can forget about that and stick with the solution Uncle Roland proposed —that Garland's remain under Jordan's wing until your brother reaches twenty-one. I know which option appears more sound to me, but I intend to offer no advice.' He folded his arms across his chest. 'The decision is entirely yours.'

Olivia leaned back in her seat and looked doubtfully across at him. If all his story about Lewis was true, then she really didn't have much choice—for if she insisted on Garland's being handed back now, who would run it till Richard was ready to take over? It would be utter madness to run the risk of landing themselves with another Lewis Ottley. Whereas, if she left things as they were, the company would continue to benefit from the undoubted expertise of Jordan management, and when Richard was finally old enough he would have a company worth taking over.

She shook her head and admitted reluctantly, 'I think it would be wisest to leave things as they are.'

Matthew nodded. 'I think you're right. Contrary to what you originally believed, I would say my uncle had your mother's and her family's interests very much at heart when he arranged the merger . . .'

Olivia glanced away. It indeed looked very much as though that were true. She had been wrong in her judgement of Roland. And even more wrong in her judgement of Lewis.

'Oh, by the way . . .' Matthew was saying, almost as though he was reading her thoughts, 'your Mr Ottley may have been clever, but not quite as clever as he thought he was. That little clause he found out about—the one that required me to marry—I'm afraid it was a little bit out of date . . .'

Now, what was that supposed to mean? She frowned at him. 'I don't understand.'

'Simple.' He paused and leaned back in his chair, watching her through lowered lids. 'That clause was removed from the Jordan charter quite a number of years ago. It no longer holds today.'

Olivia's brain was still reeling from all his other revelations. This additional piece of information was somehow more than she could absorb. In baffled silence she stared at him as he went on to inform her calmly, 'Such a restriction on the head of Jordan's was considered both unreasonable and unviable in today's more volatile marital climate. My uncle Roland had it removed more than fifteen years ago.'

'But——' None of it still made any sense. With a growing sense of dissociation, Olivia gaped across in bewilderment at the composed dark figure opposite. 'Then why on earth did you ask me to marry you?' she asked.

Matthew shifted slightly in his seat and ran a long, tanned finger down the side of his nose. 'As I told you at the time, I had my reasons. Maybe I just wanted to do you a favour. Or maybe I thought I was doing myself one.' He let out breath sharply and started to rise from his chair, sudden impatience etched darkly across his face. 'But whatever it was that possessed me, I realise now I made a big mistake.' He stood over her and added harshly, 'Since this so-called marriage of ours no longer serves any useful purpose to either of us, I suggest we take the next logical step.'

Olivia blinked, uncomprehending. 'What step?' she asked him, meeting cold, shuttered eyes.

He answered her baldly, 'The divorce.'

'Ah—the divorce. Of course.' In spite of herself, a chill went through her.

'In the circumstances, there's no reason

whatsoever for us to continue with this charade—which both of us, I think, are finding even more disagreeable than we could ever have believed.'

Olivia nodded. She could not deny that.

'Good. I'm glad I have your approval.' Matthew straightened as she glanced away. 'I suggest you speak to your brother as soon as possible. I'd like to get this divorce on the road.'

Then, with stiff, uncompromising strides, he turned his back on the suddenly limp and desolate figure sitting hunched and bewildered in the velvet armchair, and, without a backward glance, went marching out through the sitting-room door.

CHAPTER NINE

ALONE and sleepless in the spare room bed, Olivia stared bleakly into the night and tired to make some coherent order of the emotional jumble inside her head.

So Matthew wanted the divorce straight away—and surely she should be grateful for that? At least she would soon be delivered from this torment that marriage to him had become. But, illogically, gratitude was the last thing she felt. The harsh fact of the matter was that the very mention of the word divorce had been like a harpoon through her heart.

Their marriage had been no marriage at all, she was painfully aware of that, but somewhere in the midst of the upheaval it had wrought, something colossal and profound had happened to her heart. She had fought it, and then, when she could fight it no longer, had simply closed her eyes and denied it. But, finally, she was facing the truth. She had fallen in love with Matthew.

In the darkness she almost laughed out loud at the bitter irony. It had taken her a long time to come to terms with the reality that all the armour in the world couldn't protect her from the fact that, in her soul, she was a woman. A woman with a woman's needs. A woman who needed the love of a man. And the one man in the world who could give her that love was the very man she had taught to hate her.

She turned over miserably and stared at the wall, wondering in bitter remorse if things could ever have turned out differently. Perhaps if she had been less rigid, not rejecting him the way she had, they might have come to grow together and he might not be in such a hurry to offload her now. For something he had said tonight kept coming back to haunt her mind. 'Maybe I just wanted to do you a favour. Or maybe I thought I was doing myself one.' That had been his cryptic answer when she had demanded to know why he had married her. Was it remotely possible, she asked herself for the millionth time, that Matthew had actually felt something for her once upon a time?

Crazy as it sounded, what other explanation could there be? There had been no compulsion on him to marry her, and it had been his idea, after all, not hers. Whether he had hoped to do himself a favour, or her, there must have been some inkling of affection—or, at least, liking—behind the move. Surely a man like Matthew Jordan would not voluntarily seek marriage, even on a temporary basis, to a woman he cared nothing about?

Her body burning, Olivia tossed and turned. He had wanted her physically, she had always known that, just as, secretly, she had wanted him. But simple physical desire would not have been sufficient cause to catapult him into marriage. He was a man whose fundamental integrity ran much too deeply to permit such folly.

There must have been more, much more, she

realised in grinding despair. And she, like the blind fool that she was, had thrown every kiss, every gesture of affection, right back in his face.

If only, if only . . . She jammed her fist into her mouth to stop herself from crying out at the bleak sense of waste and frustration she felt. Then a wild thought made her catch her breath. Maybe Matthew still cared just a little. Maybe it wasn't too late. Maybe she could still find a way to save their marriage and stop the divorce.

But she must act now—right away. There wasn't a single moment to lose. Heart beating madly, she rose from her bed. She must demonstrate to him her change of heart. Prove to him once and for all that she was capable of being a real and loving wife.

On an impulse, she darted across to the wardrobe and took down from its shelf the lingerie box from Paris that Matthew had left on their bed that morning—and which she had never dared open since. Now, with trembling fingers, she lifted the lid and picked up the shimmering gossamer black nightie with its diaphanous matching négligé. Then, with a shiver of excitement, she slipped them on.

She glanced at her reflection in the mirror, remembering how, when he had bought it, she had believed the gift was meant for Celine. And maybe it had been, originally, but he had given it to her. Now it was up to her to lay claim, not only to the nightdress, but to her husband as well. Too passively, she had allowed Celine to take over what was rightfully hers.

No more, she decided as she headed for the door.

She must fight and try to win him back—and this might be the last chance she would ever have.

As she reached the bedroom at the end of the darkened corridor, she pushed the door open and slipped inside, trying to ignore the nerves that clutched at her throat like an iron claw. As she moved towards the bed, her eyes had adjusted to the half light and she could make out quite clearly the dark head resting against the snowy pillows, the tumbled bedclothes pushed back carelessly to expose a broad, sun-darkened chest.

At the bedside, she paused to gaze down at him, feeling her heart contract in her breast, her senses almost overwhelmed by the sheer exquisite male beauty of him. Almost reverently, holding her breath, she reached out one hand to touch the dark hair.

Instantly he was awake. With a groan he pulled himself upright and reached across to snap on the bedside-lamp. Bewildered dark eyes looked up at her. 'Olivia? What are you doing here?'

Olivia smiled back serenely, all her nerves miraculously vanished, suddenly quite certain of what she was doing. 'I come here as your wife,' she told him huskily, shrugging the black silk négligé from her shoulders and letting it fall with a soft swish to the floor.

Matthew was watching her, an unreadable expression in his narrowed eyes. But he made no move to intervene as she slipped the thin straps of the nightdress from her shoulders, so that the front slithered down to her waist, exposing her taut, excited breasts. Then, in a final fluid movement, she slid the silky fabric over her hips, stepping lightly aside to free herself of its confines and stand before him, naked and ripe.

'I'm yours,' she told him. 'All yours.' Then, with excitement throbbing through her veins, she waited for him to make the next move.

For a long, breathless moment he did not move, though she could almost feel the heat of the dark gaze that trailed lazily across her flesh. Then the ghost of a smile seemed to touch his lips as at last he leaned towards her, and, weak with wanting, trembling with anticipation, Olivia half closed her eyes and waited for the blissful moment when his hand would make searing contact with her flesh.

But that contact never came. In one movement he had reached down to scoop up her discarded garments from the floor. Then, with a harsh look, he flung them at her.

'Get dressed, Olivia,' he scorned. 'And close the door behind you on your way out!'

That was her ultimate humiliation. It was also the end of the road. The thought of ever having to face Matthew again sent shivers of cold shame down Olivia's spine.

With a resigned sigh she lifted her case from the cupboard and laid it open on the bed. She had had her answer. If he had ever cared for her, he no longer did now. Moving mechanically, she slid an armful of dresses from their hangers and proceeded to fold them and pack them away. It was the bitter morning after the night before, and she was preparing to leave St Albans for good.

As she bent to lift a pile of sweaters from a drawer, she swallowed on the hard, painful lump in her throat. Somehow the prospect of returning to her old life—a life in which Matthew would play no part—filled her soul with an agony of despair. Once upon a time that barren existence had seemed enough for her, but she was no longer the same person that she had been then.

She dropped the pile of sweaters into the case and chewed remorsefully on her lower lip. Perhaps, in truth, she'd never really been that closed-in, cut-off creature of before, only it had taken a man like Matthew Jordan to break through her barriers and defences and liberate the warm-blooded woman underneath.

But too late, alas. Right to the bitter end she had clung to her well-worn prejudices and fears, allowing her obsessive dread of repeating her mother's tragedy distort her entire view of life. And, particularly, her view of Matthew. Because he was ambitious and forceful like her father, she had labelled him unfeeling and insensitive too. Yet in spite of the way he had treated her last night, dishing out a taste of her own bitter medicine, she knew him all too well to be a warm and humorous, caring and gentle—if sometimes unpredictable —man. A man in a million, she realised now.

Pain washed through her, making her groan. If only she'd had the courage of her mother, and been prepared to take the risk that love involved! At least her mother, after years of miserable marriage, had had the guts to take a final shot at finding happiness. And had found it, Olivia felt sure. If

Roland was a fraction of the man his nephew was, her tragically brief marriage had at least been a happy one. There was some consolation in knowing that.

But what had her craven daughter done when her own chance for happiness had been handed to her virtually on a plate? First she had rejected it and then she had destroyed it with her own hands. For her chance for happiness was gone now. Forever. And it would never come again. Only once in a lucky lifetime did a man like Matthew Jordan come along.

At the sound of a car on the gravel below, she stole an anxious glance at her watch. Surely it couldn't be her taxi already? She had ordered it for eleven-thirty to get her to the station in plenty of time to catch the midday train to Chester, and it was only just after ten-thirty now.

Curious, she crossed to look out of the window—and felt her heart contract in sudden panic as she recognised the Rolls.

Her fingers clutched the windowsill as, rigid, she stood there, peering outside. Perhaps it was the delectable Celine come on some errand for her boss. In which case, since the housekeeper was out shopping and she personally had no intention of answering the door, the insufferable female could just turn right round and go back where she had come from. For the moment, at least. Once she was conveniently out of the way, Olivia reminded herself with a masochistic stab, the blonde girl would undoubtedly by given free run of the house, just as she had been given of the Regent's Park flat.

But it was not Celine. As the big car came sweeping round in a sharp curve to park below, tyres spitting gravel as it came to a halt, Olivia could see all too clearly that it was Matthew at the wheel. A moment later the driver's door sprang open and he stepped out, a tall, vigorous figure in a dark grey suit, long legs striding impatiently across the short distance to the front door.

Sudden, sharp panic biting in her bosom, Olivia jumped back from the window. What was he doing here at this time of day? Couldn't he have delayed his appearance just for an hour, when she would already have been safely gone, leaving the brief note she had scribbled to explain her hurried disappearance?

She scurried to the bedroom door and closed it quietly, anxiously consoling herself that it was really unlikely in the extreme that his unscheduled reappearance had anything to do with her. If she just stayed put and kept out of his way, he could get on with whatever he had come for and be gone long before her taxi was due. Yet her breathing was ragged and uneasy as she fumbled with the last few bits and pieces from the drawers and dumped them unceremoniously into the case. Her heart was pumping so frantically now that the noise of it almost filled the room.

At the sound of footsteps on the stairs, she clenched her fists and held her breath. He must be going to collect something from his room. She closed her eyes and swallowed drily and waited for the footsteps to continue down the corridor.

But they did not. Olivia felt her heart cringe inside

her breast as the door clicked open behind her and she heard him step into the room.

There was a short silence, during which she was painfully aware of him standing there behind her, eyes boring into her back. Numbly she forced her hands to go through the motions of arranging the clothes in her case, hesitating only for a fraction of a second as Matthew suddenly demanded in a rough voice, 'What the hell do you think you're doing?'

'Packing. What does it look like?' Her voice seemed to come from a long way away.

'I can see that.' Another pause. 'What I want to know is why you're packing. Where do you think you're going?'

'Home.' The word brought the sting of tears to her eyes and a cruelly desolate lump to her throat. Why was he doing this to her? Couldn't he just leave her to make a dignified retreat? With an effort she elaborated calmly, 'I spoke to Richard on the phone this morning, and he's in favour of sticking with Roland's plan. So you see,' she pointed out, snapping shut the lid of her case and fumbling with the zip, 'there's no reason for me to stay on here.'

A moment later her heart shrank inside her as she heard the bedroom door click shut and she could feel the raw male warmth of him as he came to stand just a few steps behind her. 'Were you planning on just walking out without saying a word?' he demanded harshly.

'I was going to leave a note.' Misery and frustration welled up in her eyes as she continued to struggle with the zip. Why was he so intent on making this so hard for her? Hadn't he already had his revenge?

'A note?' His tone was contemptuous.

What more did he expect? As the zip closed at last, Olivia swung the case from the bed. 'I think it's best for both of us that I leave here without delay.'

She felt, as much as heard, him sigh, and every muscle in her body tensed as he took a step towards her and touched her arm. 'Look, Olivia,' he said, 'I'm sorry about what happened last night.'

At the total unexpectedness of the gesture and the sudden gentleness in his voice, the tears in her eyes were threatening to spill. She blinked them back and stared at the floor. 'I had it coming,' she said.

Matthew sighed again and clasped her arm more firmly. 'No, I don't think you did. No one could really blame you for the unfortunate way that things have turned out. I'm the one who had it coming. I'm the one who screwed things up.'

It was decent of him to take the blame—proof, if she needed it, of the man he was. She took a deep breath and reassured him, 'It doesn't really matter who's to blame. What's done is done—and best forgotten, don't you agree?'

As she said it, she turned at last to look at him—and immediately wished she hadn't. At the sight of him standing there, so close, watching her through those long-lashed dark eyes, her entire being was suddenly filled with an agonising sense of loss. So near and yet so far. He was the man she had first lost and then learned to love.

As he shook his dark head, a wry smile touched his lips. 'Maybe you're right, it should just be forgotten, but I'd like you to hear my side of things first. Maybe then, at least, we can still be friends.'

She would have stopped him if she could. To be his friend was no longer what she wanted. Almost better to part in anger and bury all thoughts of what might have been. But there was no stopping him as he caught her other arm and drew her round, holding her lightly captive before him as he went on in a low, earnest voice. 'As I told you yesterday, that marriage clause of old Uncle Julius's was removed from Jordan's charter a long time ago.' A slight frown appeared between the dark brows. 'The only reason I married you, Olivia, was because I wanted to.'

She couldn't bear to hear it. So she had been right. In pain, she turned away. But Matthew was merciless as he went on, 'What's more, I never intended our marriage to be temporary. It was my hope that it would be for life. You see, I was foolish enough to believe that I might be able to make you fall in love with me. Perhaps that's why I pushed myself on you a little bit at the start. I guess I was trying just a bit too hard.' He shrugged in apparent resignation. 'At any rate, as we both know, all my efforts backfired in my face. All I succeeded in doing was to make you hate me even more than you did at the start.'

How blind could he be? The real truth, as only Olivia knew, was a million light years away from that. He had succeeded absolutely in making her fall in love with him, but, sadly, only after he had fallen out love with her. Helplessly she looked at him, bleak emotion clogging her throat. 'I don't hate you,' she managed to protest.

'Then we can be friends?'

How she hated that word! She nodded, avoiding his gaze. 'Of course we can.'

'Well, at least that's something.' Matthew leaned down and kissed her chastely on the cheek, making her bones melt and the blood turn to fire in her veins. It took every sinew of her considerable will-power to resist flinging her arms around his neck.

Then he stepped back, releasing her, one dark eyebrow raised as he enquired, 'Why did you come to me last night?' He smiled sympathetically. 'A brainstorm? Had I really disorientated you that much?'

It would have been so easy just to say yes, to make some flippant, dismissive remark. But there was something in his eyes that told her she owed him better than that. He had been honest with her; she should be honest with him. 'I came because I was hoping I might be able to save our marriage.' Pain rushed through her at the hopelessness of her words. She dropped her gaze. 'But I was too late.'

'Too late?' Matthew was frowning down at her.

'I was hoping you might still care for me.' Olivia shrugged bravely. 'But I was wrong.'

To her astonishment, a slow smile spread across his face. 'Do you really mean that—that you hoped I still cared?'

Dumbly she nodded. Vain hope!

But suddenly he was taking her hands in his, and his eyes were serious again as he chided, 'You little fool! Do you seriously take me for the sort of immature individual who changes his mind about that sort of thing?'

As he paused, she could not answer. She could scarcely breathe. Stupefied, she stared into those deep hazel eyes as he told her, 'My feelings for you are the same as they ever were, right from the very first time we met. If anything, they're more powerful.' He pulled her to him. 'I love you, Olivia.'

Olivia blinked at him. This had to be a dream.

'Why did you want to save our marriage?'

She blinked again, still disbelieving. Any minute now she would wake up. Like a sleepwalker, she opened her mouth, and then heard herself say, 'I wanted to save our marriage because I've fallen in love with you.'

What happened next was definitely no dream. The lips that suddenly crushed down on hers, sending a heatwave through her senses, were utterly, achingly, heart-stoppingly real. And the powerful male body whose arms enclosed her, locking her to him as though he might never let her go, was wondrously warm and hard and substantial, no mere fantasy of her imagining. She gasped as Matthew leaned back a little and demanded, 'Do you really mean that, Olivia?'

She smiled. 'Do you take me for the kind of immature individual who would lie about a thing like that?'

As he laughed, all the tension between them vanished. Then he kissed her face and hugged her close. 'If we weren't already married, I'd ask you to marry me this very minute!'

'And I'd accept.'

She kissed him back, then blushed a little as he teased, 'Though come to think of it, you and I, my dear Olivia, are married in name only.' A wicked smile spread over his face. 'And I think it's time we put that right.' With a lingering kiss he swept her into his arms. 'I reckon now would be as good a time as any.'

Olivia twined her arms happily around his neck, her fingers trailing through the thick, dark hair. 'I reckon you're right,' she agreed with a nervous smile as he carried her to the bed and laid her on the eiderdown. Though, as he bent to kiss her, she reached out a restraining finger gently to cover his lips. 'First, there's one promise you have to make me.'

He kissed her finger. 'Anything.'

She held his eyes with a serious look. 'From now on, no more Celine.'

At that, Matthew's expression altered. He sat down beside her and stroked her hair. 'I owe you an explanation about that as well.' Thoughtfully he drew in breath. 'I know what you think—and what I've allowed you to think . . . but there's never been anything between me and Celine.'

Olivia frowned. 'What about your affair?'

'There never was an affair—though one of us would have had it otherwise and the other one came very close to obliging. Probably, if you hadn't come along, I'd have fallen into bed with her eventually.'

'You mean you never did?'

'Never. I dated her, but that was all.'

'But what about that time I caught you together in the Regent's Park flat?'

Matthew smiled a wry smile. 'I admit that was close—but it wasn't quite the way it looked. I hadn't invited Celine to the flat. She phoned me just after I arrived . . . As you were aware, she'd been keeping tabs on me. I reckon she must have got wind of the fact that our marriage wasn't exactly a raging success.'

As he paused, Olivia nodded, remembering all those phone calls to the house, and suddenly wondering, in a flash of intuition, if they had been deliberately designed to undermine an already rocky situation.

'Next thing,' Matthew went on to explain, 'she turned up on the doorstep. She caught me at a bad moment, I suppose. I was just in the mood to drown my sorrows. And I probably would have if you hadn't turned up when you did.'

'But I thought you went after her that night?'

'Not likely!' Matthew shook his head. 'I'd already had more excitement and drama than I could cope with in one night. No, I didn't go after Celine. I checked in alone at a hotel for the night.'

Olivia felt a great weight slip away. It would always have made her feel uncomfortable just knowing that he and Celine had been lovers. 'So that weekend in Brussels really was just strictly business?'

'Absolutely,' he assured her. 'In fact, for Celine, I think that weekend was the last straw. She handed in her notice the following Monday and, in fact, she's already left.' He smiled at the look of surprise on her face. 'She's gone to work for some property tycoon in the City who's presumably a little more amenable to her charms.' He kissed Olivia on the nose. 'Do you forgive me for leading you on?'

With a smile, she pulled him to her, knowing at that moment that she would have forgiven him anything. 'I forgive you. Just don't do it again. I nearly died of jealousy, you know.'

'That's what I was banking on.' His lips curled in a Machiavellian smile. Then he laughed and nuzzled his lips against her neck as he drew himself down on the bed beside her. 'And now, before we go any further, I suggest you pick up that phone and cancel the taxi I'm sure you've ordered.

'Later—*much* later,' he emphasised, his fingers caressing the soft skin of her throat, 'you can make a call to your friend Jeffrey in Chester and tell him that from now on he'll be running The Gallery for you. You, my dear, will be staying here to look after your very demanding husband. And if you have any energy left over from doing that,' he added as she blushed with pleasure, 'we'll find another gallery for you in St Albans.' He kissed her temple. 'How does that sound?'

It sounded perfect. She smiled. 'I like it.'

'You'd also better arrange with Jeffrey to send poor old Sydney down. We can't have him languishing up there on his own. Though I warn you,' he teased her, biting her ear, 'there'll be no more private little evenings for the two of you together. From now on you spend all your evenings with me. You're not the only one with a jealous streak. I can get jealous too.'

Olivia giggled and rumpled his hair. 'Of a *cat*?' she demanded, laughing.

'Of a cat,' he assured her, smiling. 'When I said I was a demanding husband, I wasn't joking, you know. You'd better get used to the idea of devoting your every spare moment to me.'

Olivia could think of nothing in the world that could possibly give her greater pleasure. 'I'll be your slave,' she promised, hugging him.

He kissed her. 'And I'll be yours.' Then his expression sobered momentarily as he drew from his pocket what looked like a telegram and crumpled it into a ball. 'I guess I can give this the fate it deserves,' he said, throwing it contemptuously into a corner of the room.

Olivia frowned. 'What was it?' she asked.

'An ultimatum from the despicable Lewis Ottley. He's threatening to spill the beans about our marriage being a put-up job unless I agree to drop all charges against him.' He smiled thinly. 'And I was right about where he's hiding out. The telegram came from Rio de Janeiro.'

At the mention of Lewis's name, Olivia felt her stomach tighten. The accountant's callous betrayal of herself and her family was something that still hurt. But the hurt eased instantly as Matthew gently tilted her chin and gazed lovingly down into her eyes.

'It was the telegram that brought me here,' he admitted with a wry, poignant smile. 'I thought I ought to let you know in case he got in touch with

Richard.' A wide smile broke the sudden
seriousness in his face. 'But nothing Ottley can do
now can hurt us. This marriage of ours is no put-
up job. It's going to be the best marriage in the
world.' He paused. 'Which reminds me . . .' he
drew her to him and kissed her deliciously and
began to undo the buttons of her blouse, 'hadn't
you better cancel that cab?'

Somehow Olivia managed to make the brief
phone call as, lingeringly, one by one, Matthew
continued to undo the buttons of her blouse. As
she finished speaking he took the receiver from
her hand and laid it pointedly to one side.

'I suggest we leave it off the hook. A little trick of
yours, if I remember rightly.' He smiled as the final
button came free. 'We definitely won't be wanting
any interruptions for the next couple of hours—at
least.'

A shiver went through her as he pulled her
close, kissing her lips, her eyes, her throat, making
her flesh burn with excitement as, with delicate
fingers, he slipped away her blouse. Then, still
kissing her, he was removing her skirt and
divesting himself swiftly of his own clothes, till
they lay warm and naked, side by side.

As she moulded her soft, pliant body to his,
trembling and eager for his love, Olivia could feel
his hunger thrusting against her, undeniable,
urgent and strong. But his loving was gentle and
unhurried, minutely sensuous, nerve-tinglingly
thorough, slowly but surely whipping her senses
to a storm of aching desire.

'This is going to be special, my love,' he

promised her, his voice ragged and thick. 'I've waited so long for you, my darling. I want this to last forever.'

Firm, gentle fingers swept across her flesh, exploring every female dip and curve, sending glittering sensations scorching through her bones that her awakening woman's body could never have imagined.

'You're beautiful,' he told her, pausing to look down into her face. 'And every beautiful inch of you, from this moment, belongs to me.'

She sighed his name, 'Matthew, my love,' as his hands reached down to cup her breasts. Then her sighs were turning to helpless moans as his lips bent to tug at each hardened peak in turn. And she longed to cry out in an anguish of pleasure as his tongue strummed the gorged and heated buds, sending goose-bumps rippling across her flesh and desire, like a skewer, piercing through her flesh.

Shuddering, she clung to him. Surely it was not possible, she wondered, for one human being to bestow such an ecstasy of pleasure on another?

Yet it was, and she longed to reciprocate. Tentatively, she traced uncertain fingers over the hard male contours of his chest, loving the way he shivered and moaned as the heels of her hands rubbed against his nipples. Her inhibitions loosening, she caressed the sinuously moving shoulders, the broad back, the muscles of his stomach, on a voyage of exploration, like the voyage her senses were embarked on now.

'Are you ready?' he murmured as, with a deep caress, he parted her thighs. A shaft of sheer, exquisite sensation whipped through her like an electric current, sending her fingers tugging wildly through his hair and her body aching hungrily against him in response to the sweet, burning ache in her loins.

But equal to the physical sensations that seemed to tear her flesh apart was the sudden overwhelming intensity of the love that shone like a beacon within her soul. It was as though it had been smouldering in the shadows, waiting for this moment to burst into life. Waiting for this man, as she had been waiting, since the moment of her birth.

For she knew, as surely as she could feel her senses rising to some pinnacle beyond earthly reach, that this whirlpool of emotion that engulfed her was drawing her not merely towards a union of the flesh but towards some higher union—the indissoluble union of two souls. As though the two of them had been created for this moment, and for all the wondrous moments that lay ahead.

She could feel the ache in her rise to agony as Matthew paused for a moment to gaze into her eyes. 'I love you, Olivia.'

'I love you too, Matthew.' Tears of blissful happiness stood in her eyes.

And then he came to her. And at last, and forever, they were one.

Have You Ever Wondered If You Could Write A Harlequin Novel?

Here's great news—Harlequin is offering a series of cassette tapes to help you do just that. Written by Harlequin editors, these tapes give practical advice on how to make your characters—and your story—come alive. There's a tape for each contemporary romance series Harlequin publishes.

Mail order only

All sales final

Harlequin Superromance

A June title not to be missed....

Superromance author Judith Duncan has created her
most powerfully emotional novel yet, a book about
love too strong to forget and hate too painful to
remember....

Risen from the ashes of her past like a phoenix,
Sydney Foster knew too well the price of wisdom,
especially that gained in the underbelly of the city.
She'd sworn she'd never go back, but in order to
embrace a future with the man she loved, she had to
return to the streets...and settle an old score.

Once in a long while, you read a book that affects you
so strongly, you're never the same again. Harlequin is
proud to present such a book, STREETS OF FIRE by
Judith Duncan (Superromance #407). Her book merits
Harlequin's AWARD OF EXCELLENCE for June 1990,
conferred each month to one specially selected title.

S407-1

D

**Coming In July
From America's favorite author**

JANET DAILEY

Fiesta San Antonio

Out of print since 1978!

The heavy gold band on her finger proved it was actually true. Natalie was now Mrs. Colter Langton! She had married him because her finances and physical resources for looking after her six-year-old nephew, Ricky, were rapidly running out, and she was on the point of exhaustion. He had married her because he needed a housekeeper and somebody to look after his young daughter, Missy. In return for the solution to her problems, she had a bargain to keep.

It wouldn't be easy. Colter could be so hard and unfeeling. "I don't particularly like myself," he warned her. "It's just as well you know now the kind of man I am. That way you won't expect much from our marriage."

If Natalie had secretly hoped that something would grow between them— the dream faded with his words. Was he capable of love?

Don't miss any of Harlequin's three-book collection of Janet Dailey's novels each with a Texan flavor. Look for *BETTER OR WORSE* coming in September, and if you missed *NO QUARTER ASKED*...

JDJ-i